The Young

1899

By

Arthur Lee Knight

Illustrated
By
J. B. Greene

Our young rajah swung his left hand down on his right, jerked the trigger line, and. the gun roared out its tremendous discharge.

Contents

Arthur Lee Knight (1852 - 7 Jul 1944) was a popular author of adventure books in the late 19th and early 20th century. His birth was registered in St. Thomas, Devon in 1852. His father was the Rev. T. H. Knight.

His mother died at his birth and he was brought up by his father.

Around 1867 he became a naval cadet on HMS Britannia with some help by the Countess de la Warr and Admiral Sir Thomas Cochrane; a year later he joined the navy at the age of sixteen as a junior midshipman. He served on HMS Forte, a 51-gun screw frigate launched in 1858 and Flagship of Admiral Sir Leopold G. Heath who became the Commander-in-Chief of the East Indies Station in 1867 and took charge of the naval aspects of the Expedition to Abyssinia in 1868.

Arthur Lee Knight was engaged in the suppression of the slave trade in the Indian Ocean and visited far-flung places such as India, Muscat (near which picturesque port they caught a slaver with ninety slaves on board), Mauritius, Zanzibar, Port Mozambique, Cape Town. St. Helena, Ascension, Sierra Leone, Canary Islands, Madeira, Lisbon, Malta, and Venice. When in Calcutta the Viceroy of India, Lord Mayo, entertained Knight and the other officers royally, as Lord Mayo's son Maurice was also a midshipman on board HMS Forte. When the Viceroy was inspecting the convict establishment at the Andaman Islands in 1872 he was assassinated by one of the criminals.

On 13 Dec 1878 A. L. Knight married Dora Ann Stewart (1856 - 1912) in Northam, Devon where they lived. They did not have any children.

By 1886 Arthur Lee Knight had been retired on half-pay by the admiralty. During this unhappy time he decided to turn to writing and published his first book "The cruise of the Theseus".

Having been a midshipman in the Royal Navy he was familiar with the setting and the language in the navy. This made his racy and action-packed naval adventure stories realistic and readable and give modern day readers an authentic insight into life on board Royal Navy ships in the 1860s and 70s.He was elected to a Fellowship of the Royal Geographical Society on 8th February 1915. He maintained his annual subscriptions, and thus the right to use the 'FRGS' post-nominals, until his death in 1944. The Royal Geographical Society notes that "*Knight has travelled extensively & is engaged in writing on the ancient cities of Italy*".

From the Boy's Own Paper 1917:

THE "B.O.P." PORTRAIT GALLERY.

Mr. Arthur Lee Knight, late R.N.

Mr. Knight, whose serial story, "The Cayman Island Treasure," was such a popular feature of our 38th volume, has spent many years at sea. He was in the training-ship, "Britannia," with Field-Marshal Viscount French, and also in H.M.S. "Bristol." When serving in the "Forte" flag-ship, on the East Indian station, he was for three years engaged in the suppression of the slave trade on the coasts of Africa and Arabia. He has also travelled extensively in India, Ceylon, Egypt, the Holy Land, and South Africa.

Glossary

ayah – maid, amah

chowrie – a fly-flapper or whisk

coolie – an unskilled paid worker: in the 19th century this word had positive connotations, as Europeans paid coolies for their work, rather than forcing people to work as had been the case in Asia.

hawser – a thick rope or cable for mooring or towing a ship

howdah – carriage on the back of an elephant

jiggered – damned, tired out

moue – a little grimace

nuss – nurse

Perahara – procession of temple elephants

pukka – real, genuine, excellent, first-class

rum – strange, odd, difficult, dangerous

scapegrace – a mischievous or wayward person

solar-topee – pith helmet

tappal-karran – postman

CHAPTER I.

"Hurrah! we may go down to Kandy, and see the Prince of Wales and the Perahara*, Vi," shouted Oswald Cameron, a fine, handsome boy clad in Highland costume, as he ran up the steps of the broad, cool verandah of Oodoowella bungalow, in a creeper-clad corner of which his sister was seated in a capacious chair, busily engaged in dressing a doll.

Violet sprang to her feet, letting the doll fall to the floor in her excitement. "What fun, Oswald! And can we go in the bullock-bandy, and have dear old Rarmsarmy to drive us?"

"Oh, yes; it's all arranged. Mother is going with us, and father is to ride down later on."

"How delightful! I am so longing to see the procession of elephants at the Perahara, aren't you, Oswald?"

"I should think so! It is to be all quite in the dark, you know, any amount of torches and all that sort of thing. The Prince is to be at the Pavilion with the Governor, and the elephants will march in the procession right through the grounds, and be fed on sugar-cane, and then there'll be fireworks and illuminations."

*An annual festival held by the Singhalese.

Violet clapped her hands with naive delight, and then, forgetful of her neglected doll, ran away in search of her ayah, to whom she was anxious to convey the joyful intelligence of the treat that was in store for herself and her brother.

Oswald and Violet were the only children of Mr. and Mrs. Cameron, who lived upon Oodoowella, their own coffee estate, which was situated upon the southern slopes of Hantana Peak, not many miles distant from the picturesque town of Kandy, the ancient mountain capital of an extinct race of native Kings, in the lovely island of Ceylon.

At the time of our story Oswald was just nine years of age, and, though tall and strongly built, was looking very pale, the effects of an attack of jungle-fever from which he had only lately recovered. Violet, two years younger than her brother, was an exceedingly pretty child with dark brown eyes and sunny brown hair.

With the exception of one or two trips to England, the children had lived all their lives in Ceylon, although the time was fast approaching when the inevitable parting was to take place; for Oswald—who was a clever boy—was destined for the Royal Navy, and it was absolutely essential that he should go to an English school and prepare for the dread battle of examinations.

Just after Violet had disappeared, the noise of a horse's hoofs became audible. Oswald ran to the head of the steps, and beheld his father in the act of dismounting from his horse on the terrace outside. A breathless, hot Tamil, with a chowrie in one hand, was holding the animal's head.

In another moment, Mr. Cameron—a tall, fair, sunburnt Scotchman—came running up the steps. A smile broke over his face when he saw his son.

"Hullo! my young rajah!" he shouted, "I thought you would have made a start for Kandy by this time. The Prince will be dreadfully upset if you're not at the railway station to receive him. You know that, of course!"

"You're chaffing, dad, you know you are! I've a good mind to punish you by not giving you a letter that the tappal-karran* has brought for you. It's from Uncle Charlie, I'm certain, because the envelope has got the Daring crest upon it."

"Ha! then he's arrived at Colombo in time for all the festivities. What fun it will be if he can come up-country. Run and get the letter, my boy."

Oswald darted off, and his father, throwing his solar-topee on the floor, deposited himself in a cane arm-chair.

"I wish the young rajah didn't look so white," he muttered. "I trust we haven't kept him too long in this hot climate."

Mr. Cameron, being a large landed proprietor, and a man of boundless generosity and considerable wealth, had been dubbed by the Tamil coolies who worked upon his estates "the big rajah," and, not unnaturally, his little son—who was a great favourite with everyone—had acquired the pet name of "the young rajah," a title of which he was not a little proud.

Oswald brought his father the letter, and then ran off to summon his mother to hear "news of Uncle Charlie," who was really Captain Heath, of the Royal Navy, an old bachelor, and her only surviving brother.

* postman

Having seen his mother comfortably seated in a long Chinese chair in the verandah, the young rajah went and perched himself on his father's knees.

"Well, dad, what's the news" he asked, with a boy's natural impatience. "Have they any fresh pets on board the Daring? Uncle Charlie always has a whole menagerie of animals running about the ship!"

"He wants two more pets," answered Mr. Cameron, "and he expects *us* to supply them! Pretty cool, upon my word!"

"Wanderoo monkeys, I suppose?" hazarded Mrs. Cameron, with a smile; "well, there are plenty in our jungle-reserve."

"But Uncle Charlie wants half-tamed monkeys!" exclaimed the planter, with a burst of laughter, "and says they mustn't have tails! Now, what do you think of that, eh?"

"My dear Ronald, he's poking fun at you. You know Charlie's way just as well as I do!"

Oswald was laughing so that his father had to put an arm around him in order that the fate so lately experienced by Vi's doll might not befall him!

"I do call Uncle Charlie a brick, dad, don't you?" he said at length; "he always makes one laugh so!"

At this moment Vi appeared at the farther end of the verandah, escorted by her picturesque-looking, smiling ayah. The little girl ran and climbed on to her mother's lap, and was soon made acquainted with her Uncle's request.

"Not only must the monkeys be tailless," continued Mr. Cameron, "but they must be provided with so many suits apiece!"

The verandah echoed with merry peals of laughter.

"The fact is, Mona," said Mr. Cameron, turning to his wife with a somewhat graver look, "that Uncle Charlie is much concerned at hearing that Oswald has been down with fever, and proposes to take him for a short sea-voyage, which he says will set him up quicker than anything, and if we can spare our little Vi he will take her too."

Mrs. Cameron looked very grave, and clasped Vi closely to her.

"I should not mind so much," she said rather falteringly, "if I was sure it would make Oswald quite strong again."

"And I want to be a sailor, you know, mother," exclaimed the young rajah, his grey eyes flashing. "I should be very sorry to leave you and dad, but I should make friends with the middies, and learn how to keep watch and all that sort of thing. I wonder if Uncle Charlie would let me fire off a big gun! That *would* be fun, wouldn't it"

"I don't think you've yet grasped the fact," said Mr. Cameron, giving his excitable little son a pinch, "that you and Vi are the pair of half-tamed, tailless, *suitable* monkeys that are wanted to swell the menagerie of Her Majesty's ship Daring!"

There was fresh laughter at this, but as it was now time to start in the bullock-bandy for Kandy, Uncle Charlie's proposition was shelved for the time being, and the children hurried off to prepare themselves for the expedition.

CHAPTER II.

The pair of little cream-coloured bullocks trotted off gaily in the direction of Kandy, an ancient Tamil, by name Rarmsarmy, who was dressed in a white cotton cloth and voluminous turban, having control of the reins.

For the first two miles the way led through the Oodoowella Avenue, of cinnamon and lofty pine trees, which made the air fragrant with their aromatic scent. Standing out boldly against the deep blue sky the enormous cliff-themselves up in majestic confusion, their deep crevices and fissures affording holding ground for the wind-tossed areca-palms, the branches of which were alive with innumerable brown monkeys. Far away in the blue ether overhead soared a mighty eagle keenly watching for its prey.

The children clapped their hands with delight when they approached the mountain capital, for they caught sight in the distance of a gigantic Singhalese pandal, or triumphal arch, which spanned the road by which they were to enter the town. This pandal was constructed most artistically of bamboos, the openings being filled up with every kind of tropical fruit, palm fronds, and bunches of fragrant temple-flowers; but the chief attraction in the children's eyes was that two enormous artificial elephants helped to support the light and airy erection, their entwined trunks meeting in the centre of the arch. Their huge bodies were constructed of native cotton-cloth covered thickly with moss, and their capacious mouths, which were wide open, were lined with pink calico.

There is no town in the world so charmingly situated as Kandy, which, with its picturesque temple and red-tiled houses, nestles amidst forest-clad hills and groves of bread-fruit, banana, mango, and guava trees; whilst a broad silvery lake, on whose bosom appears to float a solitary palm-clad islet, lies stretched at her feet, its shores fringed in many places by feathery drooping bamboos and kitool and coco palms. In the remote distance stretch blue filmy mountains, whose summits are sometimes veiled in lazy soft white clouds.

The streets of the town were so crowded with excitable, gaily-dressed natives that the bullock-bandy could only proceed at a very slow pace to the Oriental Bank, the manager of which had invited Mrs. Cameron and her party to view the state arrival of the Prince from his capacious balcony, which overlooked the main street. Here a delightful surprise was in store for the children—the secret having been carefully kept from them—for the very first person they caught sight of standing in the doorway of the bank, with a broad smile of welcome upon his bronzed, bearded face, was Uncle Charlie himself, arrayed in full-dress uniform. It was, indeed, a red-letter day in the calendar of Oswald and Violet. Very soon after their arrival at the Oriental Bank, the Prince of Wales, in a Field-Marshal's uniform, and seated by the Governor's side, drove by in a carriage drawn by four horses, vociferously cheered by the dense crowds of natives; and our young friends did not fail to join in the general outburst of welcoming huzzas, which continued until the royal carriage had disappeared within the Pavilion gates.

Then followed tea with the hospitable bank manager and his wife and children, and afterwards the whole party—now joined by Mr. Cameron—went for a walk through the busy, festive town, in order that the pandals and other decorations might be thoroughly inspected, and also the preparations for the illuminations.

At seven o'clock Uncle Charlie took all his relatives under his wing and gave them a quiet little dinner at the principal hotel, and no sooner was the repast over than it was time to sally forth to see the great Perahara, or procession of temple elephants. Fortunately there was no moon, but the stars shone out brilliantly from the dark dome of heaven, and threw silvery reflections on the tranquil waters of the sleeping lake. The illuminations had not yet commenced, but several bonfires had been lit upon the summits of lofty peaks in the neighbourhood, the red flames standing out prominently against the dark background of sky.

Suddenly the crash of barbaric music, the trumpeting of elephants, and the excited yells of thousands of almost frenzied natives announced that the procession had begun to wend its way through the broad, dimly-lit streets of the mountain capital.

Our friends had made their way into the beautiful Pavilion gardens, and were standing under the vast branches of an old gnarled cotton-tree covered with crimson blossoms, Oswald and Violet on the tiptoe of expectation.

They had not to wait long. The deafening sounds of tom-toms, brass cymbals, and chank-shells, almost drowned in the shouts of the multitude, drew nearer and nearer, and then the torchlight procession burst into view—one of the wildest, weirdest scenes that can possibly be imagined. First came a band of masked dancers going through the most absurd steps and contortions and escorted by torchbearers in fantastic costumes. These were followed by the sacred elephants, most gorgeously caparisoned and with howdahs on their backs, who solemnly advanced with silent, measured footsteps in rows of three, a large one occupying the place of honour in the middle, whilst a smaller beast marched on either side of him, their intelligent little eyes glittering in the flaring, fitful light shed by the torches. In the howdahs, which were gay with trappings of every colour of the rainbow, sat sedate-looking, portly Kandyan chiefs, over whose heads silver umbrellas were held by attendants sitting behind them. The housings of the elephants were truly magnificent from an Oriental point of view, and they appeared to be almost wrapped up in embroidered cloths, one of which fitted over the head and covered the upper half of the long, supple trunk. In addition to this, the principal elephants had a canopy of cloth embroidered with gold held over them, which was supported on bamboo poles held by native attendants on foot. Interspersed amongst the animals were tom-tom beaters, the blowers of chank-shells, ivory horns, and other native instruments; whilst in the rear of the elephants, which numbered thirty in all, marched a body of Kandyan chiefs, headmen, and native officials, all in gala costume, and in many cases attended by native bearers in fantastic dresses, whose duty it was to shield their masters' heads from the burning rays of the sun with umbrellas of papier-maché or the broad, cool leaves of the talipot palm—the festival being usually held in the daytime, and not at night as on the present occasion.

No sooner had the procession defiled in front of the great cotton tree than Oswald, in a great state of excitement, shouted out:

"Now let's run on and see the Prince feeding the elephants on sugar-cane. Come along, dad, mam, Uncle Charlie—all of you!"

Captain Heath caught Vi up in his arms, for the party was now in the midst of a hilarious surging crowd hurrying forward to see the ceremony to which Oswald had referred. Mr. Cameron's stalwart form, however, soon forced a passage for our friends, and they fortunately arrived in front of the Pavilion—every tree and shrub near which was hung with Chinese lanterns—in time to see the Prince of Wales step forward with an armful of sugarcane with which to regale the largest elephant of the procession—a noble animal with a golden howdah on his back, in which was seated in almost regal magnificence the Dewa-Nilame, or chief lay-officer of the Temple of the Sacred Tooth* at Kandy.

* A so-called tooth of Buddha is kept as a relic at this temple

Presently the procession moved on again with all its hurly-burly of uncouth noises and its glittering pageantry of vivid Oriental colouring and confused waving of innumerable flaring torches, and pressed out of the Pavilion grounds into the town by another gateway, the medley of sound gradually dying away into a subdued roar in the distance. And now followed the illuminations, which were a source of wonder and delight to the children, and of quiet enjoyment to their elders. Every crevice in the open-work wall surrounding the lake was occupied by a tiny coloured lamp fed by coconut oil, and the dense groves of trees, which in the daytime lent a grateful shade to the passers-by, were illuminated by hundreds of Chinese lanterns of every conceivable shape and colour. The scene was one of fairylike beauty. The delicate little lamps of the thousands of fireflies that flitted about amongst the shadows were almost entirely quenched in the flood of artificial light that lit up the scene.

Suddenly a sheaf of rockets shot up into the starlit sky from the lonely islet, throwing out long lines of flame as they did so. Then, with loud detonations, these fiery messengers exploded, and the air was filled with coloured fires shooting down towards the dark expanse of tranquil water in which they were so brightly reflected. This was followed by flights of rockets soaring up from every direction till it seemed as if the very heavens were aflame. Bright revolving Catherine wheels and Bengal lights lent their aid to the general effect, and some fire-balloons slowly and gracefully ascended above the towering palms and avenues, of acacia, pupul, and tamarind trees.

It was long past midnight when the Clan Cameron returned to their mountain home, accompanied by Uncle Charlie, who had promised to spend a few days upon his brother-in-law's coffee-estate before the call of duty summoned him back to Colombo.

CHAPTER III.

It was all settled! The young rajah and his sister were to go for a short voyage in the Daring, under the care of Uncle Charlie, who, as captain of the ship, had ample accommodation at his command, the dashing frigate having been a flagship on her former commission, and therefore provided with extra quarters for an admiral's or commodore's staff.

What ultimately decided Mr. and Mrs. Cameron to make up their minds to part with their dearly-loved children was that both Oswald and Violet betrayed symptoms of fever after all the excitement of the great fete in Kandy; and Uncle Charlie protested most energetically that there was nothing like wholesome sea-breezes to utterly destroy the germs of such an insidious complaint as jungle-fever.

"You won't know those kids when you get them home again after a life on the ocean wave!" he observed to his sister at a picnic on the summit of the Rajagalla Rocks. "My little Vi shall be rocked in the cradle of the deep every night, and not need any lullabies from her ayah!"

"I thought we were *tailless monkeys*," said Oswald, laughingly, to his sister, "but now we're *kids*. I never knew such a person as Uncle Charlie for nicknames, did you?"

"Didn't you really" exclaimed Captain Heath, who had crept up slily behind the boy; and, so saying, he caught the young rajah up in his strong arms, ran with him to the edge of a cliff-like rock, and threatened to pitch him into the abyss beneath.

"*Do* be careful, Charlie!" cried Mrs. Cameron, who viewed this proceeding with some alarm. "Your foot might so easily slip."

"Uncle," said Oswald, as he was borne back kicking and struggling to his parents, "I'll always be good if you'll let me fire off one of those big Armstrong guns you've got on board the Daring."

“I’ll make you one of the powder-monkeys, that’s all you’re fit for,” laughed the gallant skipper. “You’d want a lot of drill knocked into you before you could act as captain of a gun!”

“Then I’ll make friends with all the middies, and they’ll help me to get up a dreadful meeting,” protested Oswald; “and I shouldn’t wonder one bit if we put you and the rest of the officers ashore on some desert island.”

“There happens to be a cat on board the Daring on purpose for mutineers,” retorted Captain Heath, as he seated himself on a rock and proceeded to light a cigar.

“A cat!” chimed in Vi, opening her brown eyes wide with astonishment; “has it got very long claws, and is it a Manx, like the monkeys you want so much to get?”

Uncle Charlie smiled and handed his little niece some chocolates. Then he said with great solemnity:

“Our cat has nine tails—no more and no less.”

Vi looked utterly bewildered at this, but Oswald shouted:

“I know! I know! It’s the cat-o’-nine-tails you flog the men with. I was reading about it the other day in one of Kingston’s books. But I’ll mutiny all the same,” he added, mischievously, “for I’ll never put up with being only a powder-monkey!”

* * * * * *

On a bright, fine, but a still and very hot afternoon two days later, the steam-launch belonging to the Daring shot from the Colombo pier, and rapidly glided out over the glassy waters in the direction of the frigate, which was at anchor in the roadstead, gently playing a game of see-saw with the undulating swell that rolled in from the offing, to break with a thunderous boom, in lines of creamy foam, upon the palm-fringed, low, sandy shores that stretched away for miles and miles in a northerly and southerly direction.

In the stern-sheets of the swift little steamer sat the captain, his nephew and niece, and the latter’s ayah; whilst the luggage of the whole party was piled up forward in charge of the bluejackets. Mr. and Mrs. Cameron had fully intended to pay the Daring a visit and see their children off, but at the last moment matters of importance connected with the estate had cropped up and prevented them from carrying out their intentions, greatly to the disappointment of everyone concerned.

The children had never seen the Daring before, for she had only lately been commissioned for the East Indian Station, but they had seen a great deal of their uncle, for when on half-pay he had never failed to pay his only sister a visit in her Ceylon mountain home.

The steam-launch was now within a few hundred yards of the frigate, out of whose chequered portholes the guns frowned menacingly, whilst over her stern hung in lazy, listless folds the broad white ensign of the Royal Navy. From her main-royal mast-head floated Captain Heath's pennant, and from her bowsprit the Union Jack.

"What a pretty ship the Daring is, Uncle Charlie!" exclaimed Violet; "you must be proud to be captain of her."

"I don't like her as much as the Victory though!" struck in Oswald, eyeing the frigate with a critical air, which highly amused his uncle. "Do you recollect old Admiral Drilham taking us on board her at Portsmouth the last time we were in England, Vi?"

"Of course I do; I remember it as well as anything, because Mrs. Drilham gave us hot muffins at tea, and I'd never tasted them before. And then there was that great black Persian cat that the admiral said had killed two canaries and a Java sparrow! Don't you recollect what cruel green eyes it had, Oswald?"

Captain Heath looked rather scandalised, and muttered something that sounded like "Shade of the immortal Nelson!" in his beard. Then he laughed and said aloud:

"Look here! Don't you young monkeys imagine there's a tuck-shop on board the Daring! Such things are strictly prohibited by a paternal Admiralty."

"I suppose you'll feed us on ship's biscuit and salt-junk, Uncle Charlie," hazarded Oswald, mischievously.

Conversation was now put a stop to, for the launch had glided alongside the starboard accommodation-ladder, and it was time to board the ship.

The commander and the officer and midshipman of the watch were at the entry-port to receive their chief; as also was the boat-swain's mate, who piped the captain over the side on his silver whistle—a proceeding which vastly interested the children. After introducing his young relatives to the assembled officers, Captain Heath bore them off to his cabins, the bewildered ayah following timidly in the rear, evidently much perplexed at having to descend a hatchway ladder for the first time in her life.

CHAPTER IV.

"Where's the Prince of Wales' ship, uncle?" asked the young rajah as lie pushed forward his cup for a second cup of tea about half an hour later; "I didn't see any other men-of-war in the harbour."

"The Serapis sailed last night for Bombay," answered Captain Heath. "I'm sorry you missed seeing her and the ships that were convoying her. If the Prince of Wales had only known—hum! of course he'd have postponed his departure for twenty-four hours!"

"Rather! I can quite believe that," exclaimed Oswald; "but I say, Uncle Charlie, where are all your pets?"

"Yes, where are they?" echoed Vi.

"Steward!" shouted the captain, "where's that rascal Pat?"

"He's having tea in the wardroom, sir," answered the steward, emerging from his pantry. "Particularly invited, sir, by the surgeon, who thinks he heard a rat in his cabin last night."

"And where's Peter?"

"Peter, sir, is having tea in the gunroom."

"Special invitation too, I suppose!" laughed the captain; "I hope those larky young middies of mine won't give him too much to eat and drink."

“The parrot is on the poop, sir, taking the air,” continued the steward in an apologetic manner, for he now began to feel that he was responsible for the absence of the pets on such an auspicious occasion. “The mongoose is down in the hold with the ship’s cat overhauling the bread-room for rats; and Bruin, the last time I saw him, was in the paymaster’s office.”

“Sitting in the waste-paper basket, mending quill-pens, I suppose!” laughed the captain.

“Uncle Charlie,” almost shouted the children simultaneously, “have you got a bear on board?”

“It’s only a small one,” answered the captain, with a mock air of apology, “and it won’t hurt you if you give it a quart of rum honey per day, and don’t try to make it dance a jig or hornpipe, I can promise you that!”

“Oh, send for it at once. Do let us see it!” cried Oswald, jumping up from his chair in his excitement. “Fancy you’re not telling us you had a bear, Uncle Charlie!”

“And who’s Peter? what’s Peter?” chimed in Vi; “I do so want to know!”

“Peter,” answered her uncle, who appeared to be quite calm amid the whirlpool of juvenile excitement bubbling and effervescing around him, “Peter is a marmoset monkey, and a very handsome little chap, I can tell you. Then the parrot, Boadicea, you are certain to fall in love with, for she is the very best talker I ever came across. The mongoose is called Jack, and is very fond of being carried about in the pocket of my pea-jacket. He and the ship’s cat are terribly jealous of one another, for they are both devoted to ratting, and this occasionally leads to quarrels of quite a serious nature.”

Bruin took this show of affection from a stranger
in very good part.

Tea being now over, Captain Heath took his young charges off to the after-cabin to show them a collection of Indian curiosities that he had made, and the children were examining these with immense interest when the door was suddenly thrown wide open and the steward appeared upon the scene, with the marmoset monkey on one shoulder and the mongoose on the other, whilst Bruin, the little baby bear, gambolled along on one side of him and Bat, the Irish terrier—with a comic mixture of fun and mischief in his cairngorm eves—trotted along on the other.

"Oh, the dears!" cried the enchanted Violet, running forward to greet them; "but really I don't know which to kiss first."

"Pat," said Oswald, promptly; "we knew him when he was a puppy, you see!"

But Vi was already on her knees, and flinging her arms around the soft furry neck of Bruin, who took this show of affection from a stranger in very good part, doubtless thinking it was a prelude to such dainties as buns and honey.

Oswald and Pat became fast friends upon the spot; whilst Peter, making a rush for his master's shoulder, sat there grinning and grimacing as if thoroughly enjoying the scene. The mongoose, being an extremely shy animal in society, ran silently and swiftly to the open drawer of a writing-bureau, raked a hole for himself amongst innumerable packets of envelopes, and with a thorough contempt of the ways of the world, curled himself up with the evident intention of having a good snooze, or at any rate forty winks.

Captain Heath hugely enjoyed this little scene. For days he had looked forward to the children's meeting with his numerous pets, and had rehearsed it over and over again in his own mind.

"Now I think we'll go up on the poop and see the sunset," he said at length, "and leave the curiosities till the evening."

"But we'll take the pets on deck with us, won't we, uncle?" asked the young rajah, coaxingly.

“Ob, they’ll follow us fast enough, you may depend upon that,” answered the captain with a laugh, “except that lazy good-for-nothing mongoose,” he continued, pointing to the bureau drawer; “it’s my belief he’s eaten a large rat and wants to sleep off the effects.”

CHAPTER V.

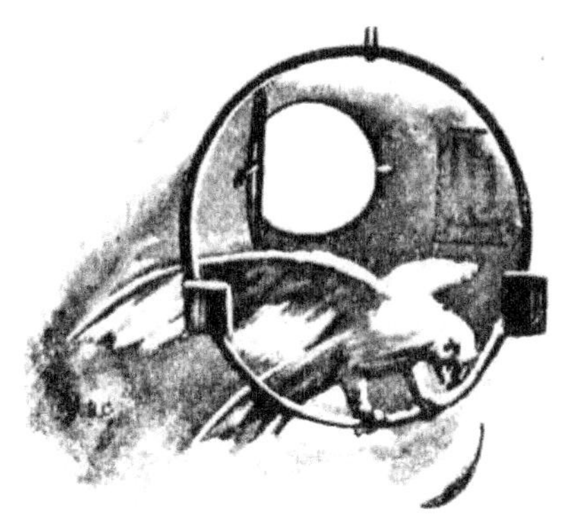

The day after the arrival of Oswald and Violet on board the Daring, that dashing frigate got under way and stood out of the Colombo roadstead under all plain sail. Fortunately the weather was delightful. The tropical heat was tempered by a cool breeze from the north, which was sufficient to inflate the ship's snowy white sails, but not strong enough to give her any unpleasant motion and thus cast a shadow on the children's happiness; although a love of truth compels me to record that the swarthy complexion of the poor faithful ayah began to assume a greenish tinge as soon as the anchor had been catted.*

During the forenoon, Captain Heath took his nephew and niece on a visit of inspection round the ship, and this was a source of great delight to them, especially the batteries of well-polished guns, and the arm-racks, the marvels of the engine-room, and the armourer's and carpenter's shops; to say nothing of the dark mysteries of the magazines and storerooms, and such novelties as the cook's galley and the sailroom.

* No allusion to the ship's cat is here intended.

Our young rajah and his sister soon became prime favourites with the wardroom and gunroom officers, and paid many a visit to those messes. On the opening night of the voyage the first lieutenant and surgeon and the two senior midshipmen dined in the fore-cabin on the invitation of Captain Heath, and this broke the ice. Oswald, especially, made great friends with the middies, and in spite of his previous threats to his uncle, did not venture to incite them to mutiny—if he did, it never leaked out, or I should have heard of it to a certainty.

Every morning after breakfast, as regular as clockwork, the children went the rounds of the upper-deck, accompanied by Ned Burton, the captain's coxswain. This was to pay a visit of inspection to the various birds and beasts living upon the forecastle, to see that they were comfortable and properly fed. This menagerie included two milch goats, Brunetta and Sylvie, the property of the captain; some sheep in pens; a number of fowls, ducks, and geese; and last, but by no means least, a pet mouse-deer belonging to the bluejackets, which was allowed at stated hours to perambulate about the fore part of the deck.

During these daily expeditions, which Uncle Charlie laughingly called "treating them to the Zoo," the children were always attended by some of the cabin pets. Pat invariably followed close at Oswald's heels, as if he was a personal attendant told off for that young gentleman's protection, whilst Boadicea was sure to be perched solemnly on Vi's shoulder, winking and blinking, and occasionally breaking out into scraps of conversation or a series of whistles. Bruin often shambled along in the rear, much petted by the seamen as he passed; and Peter, more often than not, was cuddled up in the young rajah's arms. Even the grey ferret-like head of the shy, retiring mongoose was more than once seen peeping out of one of the capacious pockets of Oswald's Highland jacket; much to the amusement of the onlookers.

The ayah—who soon recovered from the qualms of sea-sickness—often accompanied the children on this diurnal "visit to the Zoo," and her first appearance upon the forecastle created something like a sensation amongst the ship's company; the captain of the forecastle remarking at the time to one of his cronies: "Well, I reckon she be a rum un for a nuss, Bill, with all them bangles and nose-rings and other gear hanging in bights about her; and yet I'm jiggered if she don't look the lady."

"Ned Burton says as how she loves them kids as if they were her own," his mate replied, "and that proves there are warm hearts under black skins, but still it don't seem shipshape somehow not to have a nuss stow away a beefsteak and onions when the boatswain pipes to dinner."

One evening, about four days after the Daring had quitted her anchorage at Colombo, Captain Heath was seated in the after-cabin, playing draughts with Violet, whilst Oswald, with Pat beside him, was curled up in a comfortable armchair, deep in an interesting book.

"Crown that king, uncle," said Vi, peremptorily.

"Dear me!" exclaimed the captain. "You've stolen a march on me, and I shall—"

"Never say die!" chimed in Boadicea from her cage, which was suspended near one of the portholes. "Polly put the kettle on and we'll all have tea," she continued, knowingly cocking her head on one side, and then deliberately winking at her master.

"It's very rude to interrupt," said Vi, looking severely at the bird. "And you've no business to ask for tea when it isn't teatime."

"Pat! Pat! Pat!" yelled Boadicea, sidling in an excited way up and down her perch.

The Irish terrier lifted his head for a moment, glared for a few seconds more in sorrow than in anger at the parrot, and then curled himself up again with a contented sigh.

"Something exciting is going to happen tonight," said the captain with an air of mystery, as he succeeded in capturing one of his niece's men.

Oswald shut his book with a bang, and almost sprang out of his chair.

"Are we going to enter some harbour in the dark?" he asked eagerly.

"Call away the gig's crew! God save the Queen!" shrieked Boadicea.

"Speak when you're spoken to!" said the captain, sternly addressing the loquacious parrot.

"Bad little kid!" the latter snapped out promptly.

"No, we're not going into harbour," said Uncle Charlie, for the very sufficient reason that we are not near land, as you can tell by looking at the chart. I'm going to let you into the secret, and mind you! the first lieutenant doesn't even know it yet. I'm going to beat to general quarters in the middle of the night, and you'll see the guns blazing out into the darkness just as if we were really lighting an enemy's ship."

"I say, what fun!" cried the young rajah, his eyes ablaze with excitement. "Shall you fire real shot and shell, Uncle Charlie?"

"Only blank charges," answered the captain; "we sometimes fire projectiles in the day time when we can lay out a target, so as to give the captains of the guns some practice."

Oswald ran to his uncle's side.

"You'll let me fire off a gun, Uncle Charlie, won't you?" he asked coaxingly; "I'll be a powder-monkey afterwards if you like, or help to defend the ship with a boarding pike."

"What would your dear mother say" asked the captain, eyeing his nephew with a quizzical look.

"Sentry!" shouted the parrot in loud clear tones, closely resembling her master's.

The cabin door opened, and the marine who was on duty outside entered and saluted, evidently expecting an order.

The captain could scarcely retain command of his features, whilst the children burst into merry peals of laughter, which Boadicea echoed in a most ludicrous manner, ending up by repeating her favourite sentence: "Let's all have tea!"

"It was only the parrot," explained Captain Heath, addressing the marine, who, in spite of the notions of strict discipline which had been instilled into him, had a broad grin upon his face; "but as you are here, you may go and give my compliments to the first lieutenant and the gunnery-lieutenant, and tell them that I should be glad to speak to them for a few minutes."

The man saluted and retired, and in a few minutes the two officers entered the cabin, cap in hand.

"I'm going to beat to night-quarters at four bells* in the middle watch," said the captain, addressing them. "Keep it a profound secret, please, from everyone. These youngsters of mine know all about it, but they won't blab."

"The parrot may," remarked Oswald, "she's the most uncanny bird I ever came across."

"You may as well join us in a round game," said the captain to his lieutenants, "and we'll see if we can make my little Vi an old maid. Steward! bring some coffee."

"Polly put the kettle on, and we'll all have tea!" sang the parrot in a tone of exultation.

* Two o'clock in the morning.

CHAPTER VI.

When Oswald got into his little swinging-cot that night, he tried in vain to sleep. His young brain was in a whirl of excitement at the idea of the mimic battle that was to be fought during the hours of darkness, and he tossed from side to side with feverish disquietude, listening intently for the ship's bell, which was struck every half-hour, and conjuring up in his mind all sorts of visions connected with an enemy's ships, the blaze and roar of guns, combined with the clash of cutlasses, the roll of musketry, and the shouts of furious combatants. At length, just before midnight, our young hero did fall asleep, and indeed slept very soundly for nearly two hours, when he was awakened by his uncle, who, attired in a peajacket and with a sword belted around his waist, stood by the side of his cot with a lighted candle in one hand and a pair of night-glasses in the other.

"Now then, youngster, lash up and stow!" said Uncle Charlie. Our sham fight is going to begin in about ten minutes, so you'd better turn out sharp and slip into your clothes, or you'll be late for the opening of the show."

In a very short space of time Oswald was dressed, and out on the main-deck anxiously waiting for the bugle to sound. Here he encountered one of the mids of the middle-watch, who was going below to rouse out the gunnery-lieutenant.

"Hullo, Oswald," said this young gentleman, "are you going to be the captain's aide-de-camp during general-quarters?"

"I expect I am," answered the young rajah with an important air; "but I'm going to try and get uncle to let me fire off a gun. I say, Hughes, you haven't got two dirks, I suppose, have you?"

"No, I haven't; you'd better wheedle the gunner out of a cutlass, but mind you don't slash yourself," said the middy, with a laugh—and he dived below.

At this moment, Captain Heath, with Vi—who looked rather frightened—clinging to his hand, emerged from the cabin.

"Here's the young rajah, you see," he said, "as keen as mustard, and dying to get a good sniff of gunpowder."

"Aren't you quite afraid of being deafened, Oswald?" asked Vi, in rather timorous tones. "Uncle Charlie has made me put cotton wool in my ears. What do you think the ayah says, that directly the first gun fires she's sure she'll scream."

Captain Heath made a signal to the bugler, who was in readiness near the after-hatchway, and the call to general quarters immediately rang out along the gun-deck in clear, resonant notes.

Instantly the ship was alive with human beings rushing about in all directions like a colony of disturbed ants. The watch on deck were on the alert in a moment, and ran to the arm-racks, supplied themselves with weapons, and a few seconds later were at their stations, and casting loose the guns. The watch below quickly followed their example. Battle lanterns were lit and suspended from the beams. The marines, armed with rifles and bayonets, occupied the waists and poop as small-arm men. The gunner opened the magazine and shell-room, and assisted by his mates and the idlers, commenced to pass up powder and shot. The riggers got the necessary gear in readiness for repairing damages to shrouds or other ropes, and the top-riflemen clambered aloft to act as special marksmen. It was a busy scene, there being a buzz of excitement fore and aft the ship, whilst the seamen were full of dash and energy, kept within bounds by a severe discipline.

The captain took his little niece upon the poop, whither Pat and Bruin had already preceded them. Oswald, however, remained on the quarter-deck, intently watching the men casting loose the guns, and getting their sponges and rammers ready for use. Ned Burton, the coxswain of the gig, was captain of the after-gun on the starboard side, and a very smart crew he ruled over.

"I say, Ned," said our hero, edging up to him, "did the captain tell you to let me lire off this gun?"

The coxswain glanced up at the poop for a moment, and then at the eager, flushed face of his boyish questioner.

"Can't say as how he did, Master Oswald, but I reckon you could get leave fast enough if you axed him. 'Twould be a good thing if you learned how to be captain of one of these here popguns, 'cos if so be as I was knocked over by a Roosian shell, why of course you could carry on in my place."

The gun's crew tittered, but at this moment the gunnery-lieutenant gave an order for the guns to be trained on the quarter, and for independent firing to commence—the imaginary enemy being at a distance of a thousand yards.

Oswald fairly jumped when the guns began firing off their blank charges, but with all the ardour of an enthusiastic boy he hugely enjoyed the excitement of the mimic battle. And indeed the effect was very striking as the ruddy flames gushed out from the port-holes into the intense darkness of the night, and the thunderous roar of the discharges burst upon the air and was carried away upon the fleet wings of the wind. The Daring seemed for a time to be wreathed in whirling clouds of smoke, through which the guns incessantly flashed out their fiery jets. The rifles, too, kept up an almost constant fusillade.

The poor ayah, almost demented with terror, hid herself away in a dark corner of one of the after-cabins, inwardly trusting that all would soon be over; but as Peter and the mongoose—their hair standing on end with fright—shared her hiding-place, she was not quite so lonely as she otherwise would have been.

Oswald ran up the poop-ladder, and grasped his uncle by the sleeve.

"Ned Burton wants me to practise firing a gun, Uncle Charlie," he said. "You see if he was killed by a Russian shell, there'd be no one to—"

"You can't step into his shoes," interrupted the captain, "because he doesn't wear them on these occasions. However, as you happen to be rather a pet of mine, I suppose I must let you fire just one gun."

"Hurrah!" shouted the young rajah in the wildest excitement. "I say, Vi," he continued, "isn't this jolly fun? Aren't you enjoying yourself?"

"No, I'm not," answered his sister, making a little *moue*; "I'm nearly choked with the nasty smoke, and the noise is ever so much worse than I expected."

"Girls can't understand about naval actions and that sort of thing, of course," said Oswald, loftily. "Still, I'm very sorry you're not enjoying yourself, Vi," he added, feeling that he had been a little unchivalrous.

"Burton," said Captain Heath, leaning over the poop-rail, "as soon as your gun is laid, let Master Oswald have the trigger line, and show him how to fire off a sixty-four pounder."

"Ay, ay, sir."

Our hero was at Ned's side in a moment.

"Now just you stand here, my young gamecock!" exclaimed the good-natured coxswain, "and don't be afraid of the recoil of the gun, because there ain't no shot in it. Take a grip of this here trigger-line in your right fist. That's the sort! You're reg'lar cut out for a cap'en of a gun, you are, and no mistake. Hold the left hand suspended over the right, and when I gives the word 'Fire!' bring it down with a 'swish,' and off will go the gun as right as ninepence."

Instantly the ship was alive with human beings.

"And if there was a shot in it, and we were fighting a Russian,"
said Oswald, whose excitement was now at fever pitch, "I really might sink her, I suppose."

"To be sure you might," assented Ned, quite gravely; "a shell pitched into her magazine would blow her into smithereens."

The gun being now ready to be discharged, and every precaution having been taken, Burton gave the order "Fire!"

Our young rajah was quite equal to the emergency, swung his left hand down on his right, jerked the trigger-line, and had the intense satisfaction of seeing the flames leap into the darkness of the night, as the gun roared out its thunderous discharge.

"Bravo!" cried Uncle Charlie from the poop. And then, pretending to peer through his night-glasses at an imaginary enemy, he continued: "She's hauled down her flag! That last shot did it! Well done, quarter-deck quarters!"

After the sham-fight had lasted about half an hour, the bugler was ordered to sound "Cease firing!" and the men proceeded to secure their guns and return the ammunition to the magazine; whilst the riggers stowed away their gear, and the top-riflemen clambered down from aloft.

"And how glad my little Vi must be that all that nasty hullaballoo is over!" exclaimed Uncle Charlie, as he led the way down to the cabin. "Let's go and refresh ourselves with some supper, if Peter and the mongoose haven't eaten it all."

CHAPTER VII.

"I'm thinking of touching at Muscat, at the entrance of the Persian Gulf, and then returning to Colombo," announced Captain Heath at breakfast the following day. "I must say I think you young monkeys are looking very much better for your life on the ocean wave, short as the time has been."

At this moment the sentry announced the officer of the watch.

"We've sighted a steamer, sir, on the port bow," reported the latter, " and she has just signalled that she wishes to communicate."

"How far off is she" demanded the captain.

"About two miles, sir."

"Are we still sailing close-hauled on the port tack?"

"Yes, sir."

"Well, carry on for the present, and shorten sail when you think it necessary. We'll heave-to later on, and find out what she's got to say for herself."

Oswald and Violet quickly followed the officer of the watch on deck, and, jumping on a gun, gazed intently at the stranger. She was evidently a small trading steamer, and was steering straight for the Daring.

The boatswain's mate on duty piped:

"Watch shorten sail!"

"I say, Hughes!" exclaimed Oswald, beckoning to the middy on watch, "what do you suppose this old ditcher* wants with us?"

"Can't say, I'm sure, but I expect our skipper will want to swap you for a barrel of oysters if he gets the chance!"

"The officer of the watch is calling you," said Oswald, his eyes dancing with fun; "won't you get in a row just!"

* A steamer that can pass through the Suez Canal.

"You are requested not to talk to the man at the wheel or to the captain's nephew," exclaimed the middy as he ran off.

The steamer was now very close to the frigate, and the latter had taken in her upper sails, and laid her maintopsail to the mast—that is to say, she was hove-to.

The master of the steamer—which had the British red ensign flying—was now seen to seize a speaking-trumpet.

"I'm going to board you, sir," came pealing over the water. "I've something important to communicate."

"Shall be very glad to see you," Captain Heath shouted back.

A few minutes later a boat shot from the steamer's side, and pulled rapidly in the direction of the frigate. Presently the merchant captain made his appearance in the Daring's entry-port, where he was received by tile officer of the watch, and by Bruin and Pat, who on catching sight of a stranger ceased the game of romps they were having in the waist and rushed towards him.

"I shall give your menagerie a wide berth, I think, Mr. Lieutenant," exclaimed the skipper, drawing back and eyeing Bruin with some misgiving; "I can generally chum up with a dog, but a bear, to my mind, is only fit for shark's meat."

Oswald and Violet at this moment ran up, seized the two animals, and walked them off.

“So you’ve brought us news of a slaver,” said Uncle Charlie.

"Thank you, my pretty dears," said the relieved skipper. "Now I've got a rare bit of news for you," he continued, turning to the lieutenant; "something that'll put a bit of prize-money in all your pockets, and—"

"Polly put the kettle on and we'll all have tea!" called out Boadicea from the main-rigging, where she had perched herself for the time being.

"Change here for Portsmouth," she continued in her shrillest tones. "God save the Queen."

"That's a bird, that is!" exclaimed the skipper, admiringly, "worth her weight in gold she is, don't you make any mistake."

"Never mind the parrot," said the lieutenant, hurriedly; "have you brought us news of a slaver?"

"Yes, that I have. Where's your captain? Ah, here he is. Now you shall hear the yarn, and mind you, Bob Purdey isn't a chap that draws the longbow. He forges ahead fair and square under all plain sail, but at the same time always has his weather eye lifting."

"So you've brought us news of a slaver," said Uncle Charlie, as he shook hands with Captain Purdey. "Pray tell us all about it."

Oswald's quick ears had caught the word "slaver," and having left Bruin and Pat in the cabin with Violet, hurried on deck again, eager to hear the new arrival's story.

"We're from Zanzibar," the latter was saying as Oswald joined the group, "and bound to Kurrachee with a cargo of cloves and gum-copal. The day after we sailed we overhauled a large dhow running free with the south-west monsoon pouring in over her stern. Says I to myself as I took a squint at her through my telescope, 'Are you a lawful trader, or a slaver, or the Sultan of Zanzibar's royal yacht or what?' Suddenly I saw a native who was attending to one of the sails fall overboard, and a fine panic there was on board the dhow when they realised what had happened. They did nothing but scream and shriek. We were within a few cable-lengths of the dhow at the time, and so I immediately stopped the engines, and sent away a boat to search for the poor fellow that had fallen overboard. Fortunately, as it turned out, he could swim like a duck, and so was able to keep himself afloat. Neither was he bothered by sharks or any other monsters of the deep. Well, my mate picked him up, looking as chirpy as if he'd done the whole thing for a lark, and took him aboard his own craft again, which had now hauled her wind and hove-to. The captain of the dhow, a villainous-looking Arab, was as civil as could be to my mate, and thanked him fifty times over. Now Jim—that's my mate—has a smattering of the Arab lingo through our having traded with 'em so much, and he had a bit of a confab with the crew, and found out they were bound to Maculla, which, as you know well enough, is a big slave-mart. And not only this! Jim speered about, and saw in the shake of a cat's whisker that the vessel was rigged with bamboo-decks and that she had a human cargo aboard—any amount of 'em packed away like so many sardines, poor critters! Well, there you have the whole thing in a nutshell. When Jim tells me the yarn on coming aboard again, 'Look here, sonny,' says I, 'the fust of Her Majesty's cruisers that we come across on this v'yage shall get the tip from us about that slaver craft, and maybe they'll get a haul of prize-money. Now this is the tip," continued Captain Purdev, impressively laying a sunburnt hand upon Uncle Charlie's arm, "if you can cruise about somewhere in the latitude of Ras Jirdik, and keep within sight of land, the chances are you'll nobble her. She's a roomy craft, and you may be sure she has two or three hundred slaves aboard."

Oswald had slipped his hand into Captain Heath's, and was holding it tightly. He was too excited to speak. Would Uncle Charlie go in search of this slaver? Ah! that was the question!

CHAPTER VIII.

An hour or two later the Daring, with her sails furled, was steaming full speed in the direction of the East African coast, Captain Heath having resolved to capture the slaver if possible and then return straight to Colombo. Oswald's excitement knew no bounds, and his mind was almost entirely occupied by building castles in the air, in which he and the slaver-captain played prominent parts—usually ending in the capture or death of the latter. Uncle Charlie was constantly being called upon to spin yarns relating to his slave-cruising experiences, which had been fairly numerous; and when this source had been exhausted the young rajah levied contributions upon Ned Burton, upon the middies, and indeed anyone on board who was gifted with good-nature and the art of story-telling—qualities in which sailors are not deficient as a rule.

One fine morning when the Daring was in the neighbourhood of Cape Guardafui, although land had not yet been sighted, Oswald, followed by Pat, came on deck early in the morning watch, armed with a telescope of his uncle's, for he was anxious to be one of the first to catch sight of the famous cape. As the decks were being-scrubbed and were all awash with salt water, our young hero took off his shoes and stockings, and paddled about after the manner of the midshipmen of the watch—a form of amusement in which he took an especial delight. Seeing that Ned Burton was on the poop, helping to scrub the gig's gratings, oars, and other gear, Oswald made straight for him with the intention of opening fire upon a certain subject which had been agitating his excitable little brain for some time.

"Good morning, Ned."

"Good morning, sir. Come up to have a bit of a paddle this morning, and to have a squint at the land?"

"Is the cape in sight" asked Oswald, as he swept the horizon with his glass. "Uncle Charlie said it ought to be in sight by six bells."

"The look-out man ain't reported it yet," said the coxswain; "but I reckon it'll heave in sight afore we pipes to clean, and p'raps a fleet of slavers too."

"Oh, Ned, that's just what I want to ask you about," exclaimed the young rajah, edging nearer to Ned. "You really think we're going to see a slaver, don't you?"

"Well, you see, it's just this way, Master Oswald. Nobody can't say it's chock sartin that we'll overhaul any of the swabs, but there's a pretty tidy chance of it, for the sou-wester is a blowin' up the coast, and 'tis then these here cruel traders in human flesh tries to run their cargoes up to the Persian Gulf."

"Suppose there was a slaver in sight a little later on," said Oswald, looking very earnestly at the seaman; "what would you do?"

"What would I do, my young admiral? Well, I should most likely go and have a pipe on the forecastle—leastways if the boat-swain's-mate had piped to breakfast."

"But wouldn't Uncle Charlie want you to go in his gig and catch the slaver?" Oswald asked.

"Tain't usual to send the gig away," answered the seaman, who was beginning to see the drift of his youthful questioner's thoughts; "because the cutters are more useful craft for that kind of job. They're fitted with rocket-tubes, you see, and can carry some armed men in the stern-sheets."

Oswald's face fell.

"I was so hoping you'd go after the slaver," he said in disappointed tones, "and that you'd take me with you. I do so want to help fight those horrid cruel Arabs."

"Do you suppose for a moment that the captain would let you go away on active service in a boat?" asked Ned with an amused smile. "Why, I s'pose you'd be wanting to take that there Irish terrier along with you, and p'raps the bear and the parrot. 'Twould be company like!"

Oswald seemed lost in thought.

"Isn't your messmate, Manby, the coxswain of the first cutter?" he presently asked.

"That's right," said Ned, nodding.

"He looks a very good-natured man," continued the young rajah, looking wistfully at the seaman.

"Look here, my young admiral," said the coxswain, "you take my advice and watch any operations that may take place from the poop. You've got a splendid glass there to squint about with, and I'm sure your little sister would like to have a look through it now and again. If you goes away on active service at your tender years, you'll find yourself spitted on the end of an Arab spear as sure as eggs are eggs—like a chunk of bread on a toasting-fork."

"Well, I shall go and talk to Hughes," said Oswald, in a highly offended tone, and whistling to Pat, he descended the poop-ladder and made his way along the quarter-deck to the main-bitts, where the middy in question—in bare feet and with his trousers rolled up to his knees—was standing, watching a squad of swabbers.

"I say, Hughes," began the young rajah in rather hesitating tones, "aren't you middy of a boat?"

"Your humble servant is commander-in-chief of the jolly-boat," answered Hughes, who was in a playful mood on this particular morning, "and that craft is very much at your Royal Highness' disposal at any time. Let me offer you a refreshing cup of cocoa. The junior midshipman of the watch, commonly known as 'The Shrimp,' hath just made a brew of that beverage which is said to be both grateful and comforting."

"I think I'd rather like to have a small cup," said the rajah, a little shyly; "but what I want to find out," he continued, waxing bolder, "is whether you are going away after the slaver when we meet her."

"Shrimp!" called out Hughes to a tiny middy whose head at that moment appeared above the coaming of the hatchway; "a cup of cocoa for His Royal Highness the Rajah of Oodoo— — Oodoo something or other."

"Oodoowella," put in Oswald, blushing.

"For the Rajah of Oodoowella," continued Hughes, making a private signal to "The Shrimp," which the latter acknowledged with a wink. "Put in three lumps of sugar, and if you can't wheedle the steward out of some cream, shove in a tablespoonful of Swiss condensed milk. It's very fattening at the price."

"But about the slaver," said Oswald with some impatience.

"With regard to slavers," answered Hughes, pretending to draw himself up with dignity, "you may take it as a certainty that the jolly-boat will be told off for the job. The captain always depends upon me in a crisis, and I've never yet disappointed him. Still, I'll give up command of the boat to you if you wish it. Self-sacrifice has always been my motto."

"You're chaffing; you know you are!" said Oswald. "Look here! I'll tell you what I really want you to do. You've got to smuggle me into your boat somehow when we sight the slaver and you go away to fight the Arabs. I read of someone doing it in a book the other day."

Hughes gave a low but prolonged whistle, and then looked quizzically at the flushed, eager face upturned to his.

"Ah, that's just it," he said at length; "you read about these things *in books*, but they don't happen in real life, you see. Here's 'The Shrimp' with your cocoa. Peg away at it, and take a munch of ship's biscuit."

But poor Oswald looked very crestfallen as he sat on the side-tackle of a gun beside his friend Hughes, and sipped the very excellent cocoa which 'The Shrimp' had brewed for him. Nobody seemed inclined to assist him in his schemes for waging war upon wicked Arab slave-dealers. It was very hard.

Pat came and sat beside the young rajah, and nuzzled his cold nose into one of the boy's strong brown little hands. He was very fond of crunching up ship's biscuit between his sharp white teeth. "The Shrimp" had gone to heave the log. (To ascertain the speed of the ship.)

"Land on the starboard bow!" came pealing from the masthead.

The young rajah instantly forgot his woes, and—telescope in hand—rushed to the poop, with Pat scampering after him.

Yes, there was the land—a faint blue film against the clear tropical sky.

"That's Cape Guardafui," said the lieutenant of the watch to our young hero. "We shall have to keep a bright lookout for slavers now."

Poor Oswald looked very crestfallen as he sat on the side-tackle of a gun and sipped the excellent cocoa.

“Hughes has promised to give up the command of his boat to me,” answered Oswald; “that is, if I want it,” he added as an after-thought.

“You won’t refuse such an offer, I suppose!” observed the officer of the watch with a quiet smile. “It isn’t often such a chance comes in one’s way, you know! When I was your age I was at school and being rapped over the knuckles with a ruler every day of my life.”

“I should so like to go away in the jolly-boat,” said Oswald, his eves lighting up with hope again. “Couldn’t you help me, Mr. Ebden I should arm myself with a rifle, some pistols, a sword—and oh! all sorts of things. The Arabs couldn’t hurt me then.”

“Not if you had a suit of chain-armour on,” said Mr. Ebden with a laugh; “but I’m much afraid there isn’t time for the ship’s armourer to make you one! Or you might go armed like the White Knight in ‘Through the Looking-Glass.’ Let me see, he had a coalscuttle helmet, a mouse-trap, a beehive, and a few other —Hullo! where’s the youngster gone? Bolted like a young rabbit, I do believe!”

The tip of Pat’s short, stumpy red tail was just disappearing down the after-hatchway ladder, so I think we may safely conclude that the young rajah was a few paces in advance of him, making in hot haste for the captain’s cabin.

* * * * * *

“They may say what they like and do what they like,” Oswald confided to Vi half an hour later, “but I mean to go all the same.”

CHAPTER IX.

After breakfast the land was broad on the starboard bow, the Daring having altered course a few points to the southward. Oswald and Violet, in a state of great excitement, remained on deck all the forenoon, examining the coastline through telescopes, and keeping a bright look-out for any vessels that might heave into sight.

"How funny girls are!" exclaimed Oswald in an amused tone.

"Can't you shut one eye without putting a hand over it?"

"You be quiet," retorted his sister; "there are some things I can do that you can't!"

"What?" asked the young rajah, boldly, and in a very incredulous tone.

Vi remained lost in thought for a moment. Then she said:

"I can knit a pair of doll's stockings. I'm sure you can't do that, Oswald."

"I should rather think not," answered her brother, with a shade of contempt in his voice. "As if a boy would have anything to do with dolls!"

"I once saw a boy nursing a doll when I was in Paris," observed Captain Heath, who happened to be standing within earshot.

"A boy nursing a doll!" exclaimed Oswald. "Well, I never! How old was he, Uncle Charlie?"

"I think he must have been eight or nine."

"What a ninny!" said Vi with a little frown.

"I suppose a French boy might do anything of that sort!" observed Oswald with lofty scorn. "I expect the one you saw went about in a 'pram' till he was six!"

"Sail right ahead!" was sung out at this moment from the masthead.

Every telescope was at once busy, and a middy was sent aloft to report on the strange sail.

The vessel, however, was no slaver, but a French brig bound from Tamatave to Aden.

Not another sail was sighted all day, and towards evening the Daring closed the land, steering towards a huge jutting cape, named Ras Jirdik. At five o'clock she was safely at anchor in a large fairly-sheltered bay to the northward of the cape.

Captain Heath had decided to lie in wait for slavers at this spot, and so that the frigate should attract as little attention as possible, he ordered her upper yards and masts to be struck. (sent on deck) The coastline looked barren and lifeless. No native huts were visible, nor could a tree or a blade of grass be seen. The deep boom of the surf breaking on the shore could be distinctly heard, but there was no other sound except the screaming of various seabirds.

There was a young moon, which shed a faint light over the scene when night fell, but the ship's lights were not lit for fear of attracting the attention of passing vessels.

Our young rajah could not keep still for five minutes together. One moment he was hugging the bear, and whispering secrets into its furry ear; the next he was playing a game of romps with Pat, or talking the most utter rubbish to Boadicea and Peter, an insult which the former promptly resented by giving him a rather severe nip on the forefinger.

"Nasty bird!" said Oswald to Vi as the latter tied a rag—obtained from the ayah—around the maimed finger; "I didn't think she was so spiteful."

"You see, you were teasing her," answered Vi, with an amusing air of reproof; "didn't you offer her a button instead of a lump of sugar?"

"I say, Vi," said the young rajah, ignoring her question and speaking in a low mysterious tone; "I'm going to tell you a secret.

"Oh, do, Oswald dear. What is it?"

"You won't blab it out!"

"Of course not. How can you ask such things?"

"Well, look here! if a slaver comes along tonight, and the boats are sent away after it, I'm going with them."

"But Oswald, you can't. Uncle Charlie would never let you go. Why, you might be killed!" And Vi's pretty brown eyes grew a little moist.

"That's my secret, and I'm going to tell you all about it. You mustn't cry, you know; it's only silly little girls who do that! Let's sit down on this skylight. There, that's comfy, isn't it?"

"Very," answered Vi, who was nevertheless feeling very uncomfortable *in her mind.* What foolhardy plan had Oswald got in his head, she wondered, and had she sufficient influence over him to prevent his carrying it out?

"It's a regular plot," resumed her brother, "and I feel rather like Guy Fawkes, only I'm not going to blow anyone up—at least I don't think so! In a plot you must never tell many people, you know, Vi, or it'll all be discovered. So you're to hear and nobody else. You mustn't even tell the ayah. You haven't read that book 'The Nautical Adventures of Jack Brodie,' have you, Vi?"

"No, I haven't."

"Well, the plot's really in that, and I'll let you read it some day. Of course, you know," continued the young conspirator, "that all the officers, and Uncle Charlie too, think that we shall most likely catch this slaver at night-time. There'll be a frightful bustle if the boats have to be got ready to go in chase other, and it'll be jolly dark. Now do you guess?"

"No," answered Vi, "but I'm quite sure you want to do something very silly, and you mustn't."

The young rajah laughed softly, and gave his sister's hand a playful slap. "I'm going to smuggle myself into one of the biggest boats without anyone seeing me," he resumed in a low but triumphant tone; "and then I shall see all the fighting and any fun there is. That's just what Jack Brodie did, and such adventures he had, you can't think!"

"No, no, you mustn't, Oswald. Uncle Charlie would be so angry!" exclaimed Vi, putting her hand imploringly on her brother's shoulder.

"This is the part of the plot where you come in, Vi. When Uncle Charlie discovers that I'm not in the ship and gets frightened, you must tell him all about it, and say I'll be back very soon—directly the adventure's finished, you know!"

"I wish these horrid slavers would go away and not come bothering here," said Vi, in a vexed tone of voice, "then you wouldn't go making up these dreadful plots."

"If you were a boy you'd like them too, you know that," said Oswald; "but you'll tell Uncle Charlie, Vi, won't you, and I'll give you such a nice present on your next birthday."

"If you'll promise not to go, you needn't give me any present at all," said the diplomatic Vi. "I dare say you won't have any pocket-money just then."

"Oh, yes, I shall. And even if I haven't I'll make you something with my carpenter's tools."

It was useless to argue or plead with him. Vi did her best, but soon found out that her brother was in a very obstinate mood. It ended—as these matters usually did—in Oswald getting his way, and confiding all the particulars of his "plot" to his sister, who promised faithfully to preserve his secret until the fatal time arrived when Uncle Charlie should discover that his audacious little nephew was no longer on board the ship.

The evening wore on, and there was a feeling of subdued excitement throughout the ship, as if something very eventful was about to happen. Oswald and his sister were constantly on the poop, helping to keep a bright look-out, and questioning their uncle, the first lieutenant, the officer of the watch, the signalmen, and indeed anyone they could find patient enough to listen to their endless string of enquiries.

Before dark the steam-launch had been hoisted out, and the cutters got ready for service, the crews having also been warned that they might be wanted to go away on active service. Oswald had been much interested in these preparations, especially in seeing the engines and bow-gun placed in the launch, and the stokers' busy efforts to get up steam as quickly as possible.

"I shall send the launch and cutters out to patrol," said Captain Heath at length to his first lieutenant. "They might possibly overhaul a dhow that we should be unable to see from our anchorage here, and it will be good practice for the officers and men."

"Shall we man and arm boats at once, sir?"

"Yes, at once, please."

The Daring was a scene of great commotion when the hoarse voice of the old boatswain rang along the decks: "Hands man and arm boats!"

It was now nine o'clock, and quite dark save for the faint silvery light of the crescent moon, which was now and again obscured behind a drifting cloud. It was almost a dead calm in the bay, and even outside the sea was scarcely ruffled by a faint breeze from the southward.

Oswald—rather nervous now that it had come to the point—was standing in the dark obscurity of the gangway, talking to Violet, and watching the men as they rushed to the arm-racks for their weapons.

"You see, there's no slaver in sight," he was whispering to his sister, who was clinging to his arm; "we're only going to patrol, as Uncle Charlie calls it; and perhaps there won't be any fighting at all. I say, you're not crying, Vi, are you?"

"No, no," said the little girl, bravely, "of course not."

"Well, look here! Take Pat down below, will you, and tell the steward to give him some supper. He likes to gnaw a puppy-biscuit as well as anything."

CHAPTER X.

The boats pushed off from the Daring's side, and made for the open sea. The steam launch, with the first lieutenant on board, took the lead. In her wake followed the first and second cutters, both these boats being in tow of the little steamer. Hughes' jolly-boat, in spite of her midshipman's prophecies, did *not* form part of the flotilla.

During the noise and confusion of manning the boats, and favoured by the darkness—the moon being at the moment behind a cloud—Oswald had boldly slipped down into the launch and stowed himself away under a large raised platform in the bows, on which stood the nine-pounder Armstrong gun. Our hero had fixed on this spot for concealment some time before, at the time when the crew of the boat were getting her ready for service. He could not have selected a better hiding-place, as it was almost impossible for anyone to see him unless he chose to betray himself by crawling out.

After the flotilla had started on its way, Captain Heath continued to pace the poop, now turning his night-glasses upon the boats, which already looked like dark specks upon the gloomy expanse of sea; and again sweeping the distant horizon in search of a possible sail. Suddenly he made an exclamation. The large lateen sail of a dhow, looking misty and indistinct in the pale silvery light of the moon, had crept into sight around the bold, jagged outline of Ras Jirdik. The signalman caught sight of it at the same moment, and ran to make the report to his chief.

"I trust our people in the boats will see her at once," observed the captain, excitedly. "The chances are she is the very vessel we're in search of."

"It's likely enough, sir. I should say that craft is of considerable tonnage. Her hull is clear of the point now, but the light's very deceptive."

Having closely examined the dhow through his powerful glasses, the captain turned them once more on the boats.

"The launch has altered course," he exclaimed, "and is steering towards the dhow. The first lieutenant must have seen her."

"Quartermaster!" sang out Uncle Charlie a moment later.

"Sir."

"Go below to the cabin and tell Master Oswald and Miss Violet, if they haven't gone to bed, that there's a large dhow in sight which I'm sure they'd like to see."

"Ay, ay, sir."

"Those lazy chicks must have turned in, I suppose," muttered the captain, presently. "The young rajah was so keen about these slavers that I'm surprised at his having left the deck at all."

The next moment Vi, looking pale and very miserable, mounted the poop and ran to her uncle's side. She was followed more slowly by her ayah, who was as yet ignorant of what had happened.

"Well, what's the matter with you, my pretty one?" asked the captain, catching her up in his strong arms; "and where's that young scapegrace of a brother of yours? Up aloft, or out at the jibboom end, or where?"

"Oh, Uncle Charlie, I'm dreadfully afraid you'll be angry with Oswald, but he only meant it for a little fun, you know. He's gone away in one of the boats."

Captain Heath looked thunderstruck—as well he might.

"Gone away in one of the boats and without my permission," he exclaimed at length. "Pretty cool, upon my word. Did anyone know of this except you, missy?"

"I don't think so," faltered out Vi. "You won't be very angry with him, will you, uncle?"

"I suppose you were bound over to secrecy?" asked Uncle Charlie, severely. "I should like to know, however, which boat the young rascal went away in?"

"I don't know," answered Vi, clinging to her uncle. "When the men were running to get their guns and swords and things, Oswald sent me down to the cabin to give Pat some supper, and when I came up again he was gone, and the boats too."

"If any harm happens to the boy, I shall never forgive myself," muttered Captain Heath to himself; "but I never dreamed of his doing anything so foolhardy."

"Signalman!" he called out a moment later.

"Sir!"

"Have you got the signal flashing lights ready for use?"

"Yes, they're ready, sir, but I doubt if the first lieutenant could read them at that distance."

"And if I signalled to him to send the boy back," muttered the captain, "it might interfere with his capture of the dhow. It's an awkward position, very."

The poop was now crowded with officers, who had come up to watch the chase. Their astonishment on hearing of Oswald's escapade may be imagined.

It was evident to everyone on board the ship that the breeze outside the bay was increasing, for the dhow had her great sail fully inflated, and was running before the wind at considerable speed. There could be no doubt that those on board her must now have seen the Daring's boats, for the latter were only half a mile distant from her. The launch, in order to gain in speed, had cast off the first cutter's hawser, and was steaming ahead as hard as she could go, churning up the water with her twin-screws. The crews of the two cutters had manned their oars, and had their rocket-tubes all ready for use.

Oswald—little thinking that his uncle had already discovered his absence—was meanwhile enjoying himself hugely, for not only had he succeeded in his plan of hiding himself away, but had actually discovered a chink in the launch's bow timbers through which he was able to peep and see to a certain extent what was going forward—a chance which he had never expected to get.

I trust my young readers are not sympathising with the hero of this story in his escapade. For my part I think he was—although a jolly little fellow in most ways—a very naughty boy to become a stowaway in the launch, and I cannot help hoping that his uncle will administer a good wigging to him the instant that he returns to the ship. The service would go to the dogs, you know, my young friends—if you don't know it, you can take my word for it—if this sort of thing was not instantly put a stop to.

From his friendly chink Oswald could see in a very indistinct fashion that the dhow was doing her best to escape from the pursuing launch. Her lofty cotton sail looked very ghostly in the dim, silvery light of the moon, which also shed a narrow pathway of beams along the surface of the dark rippling sea. The breeze, though not strong, was quite enough to fill the tall lateen sail, and the dhow swept along at a steady six or seven knots an hour, heading almost due north-east and paying no attention whatever to the man-of-war's boats.

"We must send a shot across that fellow's bows," exclaimed the first lieutenant at length, "or he may escape us."

"You may depend upon it she's a slaver, sir," observed the coxswain, who was perched up in the stern-sheets, steering: "or she wouldn't be so anxious to show us a clean pair of heels."

"I must own I think she's a suspicious-looking craft," assented the lieutenant. "No doubt she is the very slaver we're in search of."

"A bit of a scrimmage will suit us very well," said the seaman with a grin, "especially if there's a haul of prize-money at the end of it. A few dollars never come amiss to Jack, I reckon!"

"We'll fire a blank charge first," said the lieutenant, "and see if the dhow's skipper will take a gentle hint. If he doesn't we must give him a *broad* one in the shape of a nine-pounder shot."

These observations were overheard by our young stowaway in his hiding-place, and they disturbed him not a little, for it suddenly occurred to him that the Armstrong gun was immediately over his head, and that its discharge would probably half deafen him, especially when shot or shell was being used. And again the gun might come crashing through its own platform owing to the force of the explosion and crush him just as if he was a mere cockroach. These ideas sent a chill through him and he began to wonder whether or not he had been foolish to choose such a hiding-place.

"Shove a blank cartridge into that gun and fire it!" ordered the lieutenant in peremptory tones.

One or two of the gun's crew sprang forward and began to carry out this order. Oswald—his nerves at a great tension—

stuffed his fingers into his ears and awaited in dread the discharge of the little ordnance. *Bang*! a jet of flame had gushed from the gun's mouth and a wreath of grey smoke was being drifted away to leeward on the wings of the wind.

Directly the noise of the report had died away, Oswald removed his fingers from his ears and applied his eye to his friendly chink. There was the dhow still rushing along with her ghostly sail outspread, quite ignoring the peremptory signal she had received. Our hero even fancied that he could perceive the swarthy faces of several Arabs looking contemptuously over the vessel's side; but there was probably a good deal of imagination in this.

To a certain extent the launch had intercepted the dhow, but when the latter, on perceiving the boats, altered course to the northeast it became a chase pure and simple. The launch was a very fast boat, but it was doubtful if she could overhaul a swift dhow if the latter had a strong and favourable breeze to run before. And there was no question about it, the breeze was freshening every moment, which was an encouragement to the wily Arabs to crack on sail.

"An obstinate fellow!" exclaimed the lieutenant when he perceived that his summons to heave-to was disregarded; "and must have a very good reason for wanting to evade us. Shove a shot in the gun next time, and try to wing her. Aim at her mast."

Oswald curled himself up with his fingers in his ears in the darkest corner of his hiding-place'. This constant firing just over his head was not at all to his taste.

Once more the sharp report of the gun rang out—more ear-piercing than before—and a tiny shot went rushing through the air; but instead of hitting the dhow's mast, it tore a hole through her sail, and then pitched into the sea on the other side of the vessel, throwing up jets of spray as it did so.

“Good shot!” cried the lieutenant,
with a ring of enthusiasm in his voice.

Oswald could not watch the flight of this shot, for the smoke obscured the view.

The dhow still held on in a grim, determined way. Her crew was evidently a very brave or a very apathetic one.

"I believe we're slowly creeping up, coxswain, in spite of the freshening breeze," observed the lieutenant, who was intently watching the dhow through his night-glasses; "what do you think?"

"Yes, I think we are, sir. Our engines are working splendidly."

"We must try another shot at her. Better luck next time perhaps, eh?"

The moon had now become obscured behind some driving clouds, and the dhow did not present such a good target as she did before. The cutters had hoisted their lugsails to the favourable breeze, and were spinning along at a great pace, though at some distance astern of the launch.

Again the Armstrong gun sent its iron messenger hurtling through the air; but this time, owing to the deceptive light, the shot splashed into the water astern of the dhow, although so close to the vessel that some of the spray flew in over her taffrail.

The cloud passed away from the moon, and once more the high-pooped stern and gleaming sail of the dhow became faintly visible like those of a spectral ship sailing over a spectral sea.

Bang! For the fourth time a shot went hissing on its way, and this time it went well home, and struck the dhow's mast fair and square, bringing it down in a perfect wreck, rendering the vessel quite helpless and terribly hampering her deck.

"Good shot!" cried the lieutenant, a ring of enthusiasm in his voice; "she can't possibly escape us now."

"Well, I hope that horrid gun will be quiet now," thought Oswald, who was straining his ears to catch the officer's remarks. "Now if they'll only rush furiously up the dhow's side and carry her by boarding, like Nelson used to treat the

Frenchmen, I shall be as happy as a king; only I must take care not to venture out and show myself, or I really do believe the first lieutenant would have a fit."

The confusion that reigned on board the unfortunate dhow was very great, and the shouts and cries of the natives on board her could be plainly heard. It was evident that they were doing their best to clear away the wreck of the mast and yard before the man-of-war's boats could reach them.

The launch rushed on at full speed, a little wave piled up at her bows.

Oswald kept his eyes at the chink, and eagerly watched everything that was going forward on board the dhow. His heart was beating so fast he could hear its thumps.

The cutters were still some way astern, but were sailing bravely on in support of their consort.

The supreme moment was at hand.

Was the vessel a slaver, and if so, would her crew show fight? That was the question.

"Be ready to board, my lads!" called out the lieutenant, as he buckled his sword-belt on tightly. "We shall see in a moment if the rascals have slaves on board."

The seamen were all ready for conflict if it should prove necessary. There was still a chance, however, that she might prove to be a lawful trader, though her strenuous efforts to escape certainly bore an ugly look.

"I wish I was a midshipman, and could board too," muttered Oswald, who was now in a perfect fever of excitement. "I wonder if the Arabs will fire muskets and pistols at us. They will, I suppose, if they're angry, and they must be angry from the dreadful noise they're making."

"Stand by, lads," sang out the lieutenant in warning tones. "Easy ahead with the engines. Not a blow is to be struck, remember, without orders from me."

Scarcely had these words escaped the officer's lips than several long musket barrels were protruded over the dhow's port bulwarks and stern, and little jets of flame darted from the muzzles, followed by puffs of grey smoke. Then *ping-ping* sang some bullets close over the heads of the launch's crew.

"She's a slaver," shouted the lieutenant. "Give her a volley, marines. Stand by to follow me on board, lads. Stop the engines."

CHAPTER XI.

Four marines who were in the stern-sheets of the launch poured in a volley from their rifles just before the little steamer glided along-side the dhow, but whether their shots took effect or not it was impossible to say, for both vessels were now enshrouded in smoke. The Arabs kept peppering away with their long guns, but their aim was very bad, and not a single man in the British boat was hit. To a certain extent the slaver's crew had cleared away the wreck of their fallen mast, but their deck was still a scene of great confusion.

A loud and melancholy wail of terror ascended from the bamboo decks below, which was distinctly heard above the din and turmoil of the conflict. These were the frightened cries of two hundred and sixty miserable slaves who were pent up, half starved and half suffocated, and who, unaware that their rescuers were at hand, imagined that some fresh and terrible fate awaited them—an idea which the cruel Arabs took care to foster.

The instant that the launch glided alongside the dhow some of the seamen busied themselves in lashing her securely to the larger vessel, which fortunately they found no trouble in doing. This enabled everyone except the stoker to join in the boarding operations, for as the cutters had not yet arrived upon the scene the British sailors were greatly outnumbered by their swarthy opponents, and every man was of importance.

In spite of his fear of being discovered Oswald could not resist the temptation of peeping out from under the gun-platform. Just at this critical moment, however, there was little chance of his being observed, for the lieutenant, sword in hand, was already clambering up the slaver's side, closely followed by his devoted men. The moon had once again become obscured, and the gloom that prevailed was only broken by the red flashes that issued from the muzzles of muskets and pistols.

A short but stubborn fight took place on the deck of the dhow, for the Arabs had a valuable cargo of slaves on board and were not likely to yield them up without a desperate struggle. Their captain owned a great many of the slaves, and had hitherto been very successful in evading the British cruisers employed on the East Coast of Africa. The ferocious bravery of this man and his crew was, however, more than balanced by the steady discipline and superior weapons of the bluejackets, and they soon had to give way before them. The cutters' crews, too, very shortly reinforced the launch's men, and the numbers were then more than equalised.

Having had several of their men wounded, and seeing that their case was a desperate one, the Arabs at length threw down their weapons and begged for mercy. Their wily captain, however, not relishing the idea of captivity—which he fancied awaited him—managed to effect his escape in one of his own boats which was towing astern; and in this flight he was accompanied by two of his leading adherents.

The remainder of the Arabs were quickly disarmed and taken prisoner, and then it became the very pleasant duty of the first lieutenant to inform the numerous slaves that they were free. This was done by means of a native interpreter belonging to the Daring, who had accompanied the expedition in the launch. The joy of these poor creatures when they heard the welcome news was unbounded, for they had fully thought that they were only exchanging one set of cruel taskmasters for another.

The Arabs kept peppering away with their long guns.

Taking the prize in tow, the launch slowly steamed back into the bay where the Daring lay at anchor, the cutters having made fast to the stern of the dhow. Three or four of the seamen had been slightly wounded in the affray, but by great good fortune nobody had been killed on either side. The Arabs had had eight or nine men wounded, two of them rather severely.

Captain Heath was greatly relieved when he saw the launch approaching with the other craft in tow, but be was still anxious to obtain immediate news of the safety of his scapegrace nephew, for the sounds of the conflict had been indistinctly heard on board the Daring, and he was haunted by the idea that a stray bullet might have struck the boy if he had foolishly exposed himself during the fight.

Vi, with her hand tightly clasped in her uncle's, was standing by the entry-port when the boats came alongside. Captain Heath started forward as the first lieutenant ran up the side.

"You've got my boy safe and well, of course," he cried. "We've been terribly anxious about the young monkey."

"Boy! what boy, sir?" demanded the astonished lieutenant.

A bewildered look crossed the captain's face for a moment.

"Oh, he's in one of the cutters, I suppose," he said, hastily. "Have you seen nothing of my nephew Oswald? He stowed himself away in one of the boats whilst the expedition was being prepared."

The pallor of the lieutenant's face could be seen even in the indistinct light that prevailed, and it was in a decidedly alarmed tone that he replied:

"We've seen nothing whatever of him, sir, but he may still be hidden away in one of the boats, though I feel sure that he could not have been in either of the cutters without being discovered. I'll have the launch thoroughly searched, for the youngster may be afraid of the reception you are likely to give him after such an escapade."

The coxswain and crew of the launch immediately set to work to search the boat, their suspicions at once falling upon the gun-platform as the most likely place of concealment; but no Oswald could be found, and the men all gave it as their emphatic opinion that he had never been in their boat at all, and must have stowed himself away in one of the cutters in some ingenious way.

The two latter boats had been busily employed in anchoring the slaver, but they now came alongside the Daring and were immediately searched, with the same result. The missing boy was not discovered in either of them, and the officers agreed with the lieutenant that they should inevitably have seen him had he attempted to conceal himself in such small open craft as theirs.

Captain Heath's heart sank within him. What terrible late had overtaken this plucky but wilful boy whom he loved as dearly as if he had been his own son? Could the youngster have been playing them all a practical joke and be hiding away somewhere on board the Daring? It seemed very improbable, but still no one had seen him go down into the boat, and it was just a faint hope.

CHAPTER XII.

The tearful and frightened Vi would not allow that there was any chance of her brother being on board the Daring. She was positive that he had gone in one of the boats, and we know that she was right.

The search parties were baffled at every point. Uncle Charlie himself narrowly examined the launch by the aid of a lantern, and even boarded the slaver and searched her from stem to stern. The launch, too, was sent to scour the waters of the bay—all with no result. The disappearance of the boy was a terrible mystery. There seemed no clue—no hope. Nobody attempted to sleep that night; the anxiety was too keen. Officers and men alike were seized with melancholy forebodings.

The pale yellow dawn of a tropical morning broke over the expanse of the broad and tranquil bay, illuminating with a pale glow the bold serrated brow of Ras Jirdik.

A native boat glided suddenly into view around the point. Four natives provided with paddles were seated in her, and made their little craft fly along at a great pace. In guttural tones they conversed in an excited manner.

The signalman soon perceived the boat, which was evidently steering for the Daring. In a moment the news flew like wildfire through the ship that a native craft was approaching. Could her occupants possibly have any news of Oswald, or were they only coming off to sell fish?

With a pale, disturbed face Captain Heath watched them narrowly through his telescope. No, most decidedly there was no boy in the boat.

When the little craft came alongside, the Daring's port-holes were black with men's heads and the quarter-deck was crowded with officers in various stages of undress.

Two of the natives ran up the side, and were met at the entry-port by the anxious captain and several of the senior officers. The interpreter was in attendance in case his services should be required.

The story the black messengers brought was short but of enormous importance. They had been ordered, they said, by the Arab captain of the captured dhow to go on board the Daring and inform her captain that he had as captive a white boy who had been taken prisoner during the conflict. This boy the Arab captain declared would only be restored on condition that a ransom of £200 in English gold was paid over to him, and that his crew were released. The dhow and the slaves he did not dare to ask for, knowing that it would be useless.

How great was the joy of everyone on board the Daring when the news became known that Oswald was alive, and likely to be restored to them.

A light broke in upon the first lieutenant when the interpreter had finished his translation of the natives' story. He remembered how the captain of the dhow had managed to escape in a boat with some of his men, and was now forced to the conclusion that these audacious fellows must in some way have managed to kidnap the stowaway. *How* it could have been done he could not imagine.

Captain Heath was only too eager to come to terms with the Arab captain. He gave presents of knives and bead ornaments to the messengers—who belonged to a Somali tribe—and told them to return with all speed to their employer and inform him that if the boy he held captive was at once returned, he should not only have the ransom of £200 paid over to him, but should also receive back his crew and a goodly number of presents of a more or less substantial nature. There was one condition which Captain Heath insisted upon, and that was that the Arab skipper should never again take part in the vile slave trade, and he sent word to the Arabs that they would have to sign a document to this effect.

Before noon the young rajah was in his uncle's strong, loving arms—none the worse for his extraordinary adventure. As for Violet, who had been suffering tortures of anxiety, her joy knew no bounds, and there was general rejoicing fore and aft the ship. The Arab captain brought his captive on board the Daring, and was duly rewarded by the payment of the ransom and the release of his crew.

The Daring took all the slaves on board and sailed immediately for Aden, with the dhow in tow, she being afterwards used as a target and sunk.

"There is no question about it, I ought to give you a most tremendous wigging, young man," said Captain Heath, as soon as he found himself alone in the cabin with his nephew and niece. "You've given us all a most terrible fright through your thoughtlessness."

"One of the Arabs got a grip of me."

"I'm really very, very sorry," said Oswald penitently, "but I thought it would be such fun to have the same adventures as Jack Brodie, and after all they weren't the same one bit. You'll forgive me, won't you, Uncle Charlie? Oh, those Arabs *did* give me a fright."

"If your adventures were not the same as Jack Brodie's, I should very much like to know *what* they were," said Uncle Charlie, after looking severely at his nephew for some minutes. "We've had no explanation of your disappearance yet, and should like uncommonly to hear the story. Come, out with it."

"Yes, do tell us, Oswald," chimed in Vi, as she curled herself up in a big armchair to listen, "and then you'll have to go down into the gunroom and spin the yarn—as they call it—to the middies. Hughes made me promise."

"Well, this is how it all happened," said the young rajah, sitting down and taking Pat on his lap; "you know that I hid myself away under the gun-platform in the launch. When the first lieutenant and his men rushed up the slaver's side, I was very nearly following them, I was so excited. There was no one left in the boat except the stoker, but I was afraid to show myself even to him, for fear he should call the lieutenant and tell him. I heard all the noise of the fighting going on and wondered which was getting the best of it, though I guessed, of course, that our fellows would lick the Arabs. After a time I saw the stoker go aft and begin rummaging about in a locker, so whilst his back was turned I slipped out to have a look round. Just at that moment an Arab boy fell overboard from the slaver and splashed into the water close to the bows of the launch. He was wounded and couldn't swim one bit, so I got up in the bows of the launch, thinking I might be able to reach down and save him. There was such a fearful noise on board the dhow that the stoker didn't hear me clambering about, and he couldn't see me with his back turned. I leaned over and thought I had got hold of the Arab boy's hand, but somehow I was so excited and in such a hurry that I overbalanced myself and fell overboard. I was in a fright when I tumbled in, but still you know I can swim a little. Before I had any time to think about it, though, I felt somebody grip me by the arm, and the next moment I found myself lying in a boat, held down by a horrid, scowling Arab. On a seat close by was the boy I had tried to save, for they had lugged *him* in too. Two other Arabs were pulling the oars as hard as they could, and we seemed to be making for the shore. I couldn't speak or shout, for the Arab held me by the throat. I wondered if any of the officers or sailors had seen what had happened and would come in a boat after us.

"By-and-by I knew it was no good hoping for this, and then we got into tremendous great breakers close to the beach, and we were all washed out of the boat, and really I thought I was going to be drowned, but one of the Arabs got a grip of me and swam with me through oh! such enormous seas, and we got thrown up on the beach jolly well out of breath and bruised. I think another Arab helped the wounded boy. I fancy the boat was smashed.

"The Arabs went off up the cliffs and took refuge in a big cave where we found several black men sitting round a fire. There was a tremendous lot of talk between these men and the Arabs, and they all looked at me as if I was a wild animal at the Zoo. They didn't hurt me, though, and I was allowed to sit near the fire and dry myself. One of the black men gave me a round white cake to eat, but it was nasty just. An hour or two later some of the natives left the cave, but they came back again in the early morning and had another talk with the Arabs. Then they gave me some milk, which wasn't half bad and some bananas; and as soon as I had finished the Arabs signed to me to follow them and left the cave. They took me straight down to the beach, where there was a boat waiting. We all got in and then shoved off through the surf, which I thought every moment would swamp the boat. However, we managed all right, and wasn't I jolly glad just when I saw that we were steering for the Daring. That's all the story, Uncle Charlie."

"It was very plucky of you to try and save the life of that wounded Arab boy," said Captain Heath, "and in consideration of that you have my free forgiveness for your escapade. But you must promise me, my boy, that you won't do anything so stupid and so thoughtless again."

"Indeed I won't," said the young rajah, running to the captain and kissing him. "You're the dearest and best of uncles. Aren't you?"

"I don't know about that," answered Uncle Charlie, laughing.

"Oh, but we do," cried the children in a chorus, in which Pat joined with vociferous barking.

* * * * * *

The Daring landed her slaves at Aden and then returned straight to Colombo. Uncle Charlie took his little nephew and niece at once up-country and restored them to their father and mother looking the picture of health and happiness. Mr. and Mrs. Cameron looked somewhat grave when they heard the story of the young rajah's adventure with the slaver captain, but they came to the conclusion in the end that "all's well that ends well."

The parting with the numerous pets on board the Daring was quite a trial to Oswald and Violet. Really it was quite pathetic.

As the steam launch left the ship to convey them ashore Boadicea, who was perched in the main rigging with her head very much on one side, shrieked out: "Good-bye! God save the Queen!"

NOTES

HMS Forte

HMS Forte was a Royal Navy mixed propulsion propeller frigate that operated as a flagship at various British naval stations in the Atlantic from the mid-19th century until 1872.

HMS Forte, the third ship of that name in the British Navy, was launched on 29 May 1858 at Deptford Dockyard.

Wooden-hulled, she was 64.6 m long, 15.2 m wide, 3456 tons displacement, and had a crew of 515 men. She was a mixed propulsion ship, with a frigate rig and a steam engine driving a propeller. She carried 51 guns.

Between 25 January 1860 and June 1861, under the command of Captain Edward Winterton Turnour, she was assigned to the Cape of Good Hope as the flagship of Rear-Admiral Henry Keppel. She sailed from Sheerness on 30 April and arrived at Table Bay on 22 September. After rounding the Madebourg and Simon's Bay coasts on 2 January 1861, she began a new tour of the southwest coast and Ascension Island.

In June 1861 Keppel transferred her ensign to HMS Emerald and sailed back to England. Between then and November 1862, under the command of Captain Thomas Saumarez, she operated as Rear Admiral Richard Laird Warren's flagship off the south-east coast of South America. There, the arrest of three of its officers was one of the main triggers of the so-called Christie Question, a serious conflict that led to the breakdown of diplomatic relations between the Brazilian Empire and Great Britain.

Between 12 November 1862 and 8 September 1864, she remained in a similar capacity but under the command of Captain Arthur Mellersh, operating between Rio de Janeiro, the Rio de la Plata and the Falkland Islands.

Beginning her return to Great Britain, on 12 July 1864 she arrived at Bahia, on 9 August at Fayal, at Portsmouth on the 28th and finally stationed at Sheerness.

Between 21 August 1868 and the end of 1869, under the command of Captain John Hobhouse Inglis Alexander, she served as flagship of Commodore Leopold George Heath at the East Indies Naval Station.

In September 1870 she passed to the command of Captain Arthur Mellersh, remaining in a similar capacity, this time under the flag of Rear-Admiral James Horsford Cockburn.

She served her last commission for the Royal Navy in 1872, passing to Chatham (Kent), where she underwent modifications in 1879 for transport duties, and in 1894 she was converted to serve as a coal depot. On 23 November 1905 she burned while in port with 1800 tons of coal on board and was sunk by boats from the torpedo training ship HMS Acteon to prevent the fire from spreading.

Language and Race

Sometimes the past is difficult to understand, because words change their meanings. Take a simple word such as *nice*. When someone tells you that you are a *nice person* you will probably be pleased. Back in the 14th century you would have reacted very differently as *nice* meant *foolish, silly, simple* or *ignorant.*

Arthur Lee Knight used language the way it was understood in England in the second half of the 19th century, so when reading his books it is important to know how words were understood at the time, especially when this involves words that involve racial sensitivities. In the 19th century the term *black* was often considered to be offensive, whereas *Negro* was the polite, politically correct term of the day, a usage that continued until the 1960s when Martin Luther King used the term *Negro* in his famous speech "I have a dream".

A much more contentious term is what is often just referred to as the *N-Word.* According to Wikipedia: "In the English language, the word *nigger* is an ethnic slur used against black people, especially African Americans."

The term originates from the Latin *niger* meaning *shiny black*, as opposed to *ater* referring to a dull *black colour*. At a time when Latin was still the international language and the use of Latin words in English was popular, *niger* also entered the language, at first without any of the connotations it has today. Especially in American English the word underwent numerous changes in meaning and spelling (niggur, nigga) and slipped back and forth from derogatory to endearing. By the second half of the 19th century nigger was used as an offensive word in American English, whereas in British English it was used to describe dark-skinned people in general, including those from India, Malaya and elsewhere, without the negative connotations it had in America. An example of this is a book by Joseph Conrad who is still famous for *Heart of Darkness*. In 1897 he published *The Nigger of the Narcissus*, but in the USA the title was changed to *The Children of the Sea*. So when a character in one of Arthur Lee Knight's stories uses the term *nigger*, it would have been understood as a neutral term. The African nations of Nigeria and Niger continue to have names deriving from the Latin *niger* to this day.

A word that could be misunderstood is *nigrescent* meaning *blackish, dark* from the Latin *nigrescere* to grow black. This now rare word is not linked to matters of race, but is used to describe natural phenomena.

Piccaninny is a word applied originally by people of the West Indies to their babies and more widely referring to small children, as in Melanesian Pidgin. It is a pidgin word form, derived from the Portuguese pequenino "very small". In the 19th century it was also used to describe small objects and children of any colour. In contrast to this neutral meaning, the word has been used in North America as a racial slur referring to a dark-skinned child of African descent.

Demands to censor old books are not infrequent such as with the famous "Huckleberry Finn" which contains the word "nigger" around 200 times. To censor or bowdlerize texts is nothing new. In 1807 Thomas Bowdler — an English doctor, whose name gave us the verb bowdlerize — published an expurgated edition of Shakespeare, which he claimed would be more appropriate for women and children than the original, with its bawdy and sexual language.

Attempts to sanitize classic literature have a long, sad history. Chaucer's "Canterbury Tales", Roald Dahl's "Charlie and the Chocolate Factory" and other famous pieces of literature have been challenged or have suffered at the hands of uptight editors. There have even been purified versions of the Bible to remove sex and violence!

The patronizing Big Brother aspect of these literary fumigations is sadly reminiscent of an Orwellian world. We, the censors, need to protect you, the naïve, delicate reader. We, the editors, need to police writers (even those from the past), who might have written something that might be offensive to someone sometime.

Authors' original texts should be sacrosanct intellectual property, whether a book is a classic or not. Tampering with a writer's words underscores an editor's extraordinary arrogance and intolerance.

Slavery

Slavery predates written records and has existed in most cultures.

Slavery was widespread in Africa, which pursued both internal and external slave trade. Some 13 million Africans fell victim to the transatlantic slave trade, while the islamo-arabic slave trade caused at least 17 million Africans to be enslaved.

At the time of Arthur Lee Knight the Royal Navy was actively engaged in suppressing the Islamic slave trade in the Indian Ocean, which was part of the most widespread global system of slavery that lasted for over a thousand years, a system that had ravaged most of Africa and prevented the rise of any non-muslim society and culture.

When, in the wake of the conquests, an Islamic culture emerged in the Middle East, Islamic theorists justified slavery on a "scientific basis". For the first time, they developed a real racism of skin colour. An anonymous author from Iraq (c. 902) attributes the emergence of different races of deficient subhumans to climate; in the hot climatic zone the children would be "cooked" in the womb for too long; "*so that the child falls between black and dark, between foul-smelling and stinking, curly-haired, with uneven limbs, defective mind and depraved passions, such as the Zanj, the Ethiopians and other blacks who resemble them*".

A Persian geographical treatise (982 AD) asserts:

"*As for the countries of the south, all their inhabitants are black...They are people who do not meet the standard of humanity*".

Similarly, the geographer Maqdisi (1st century) notes about Black Africans:

"*There are no marriages among them; the child does not know its father; and they eat people .... As for the Zanj (East Africans south of Ethiopia), they are people of black colour, flat noses ... and low intelligence*".

Arab philosophy adopted this skin-colour racism. Thus, the great Avicenna (Ibn Sina, d. 1037) underpinned the Aristotelian theory of the subhuman with climate theory; extreme climates produced slaves by nature: "*for there must be masters and slaves*"; and in the Liber Canonis he asserted that black Africans were intellectually inferior. This racial theory was also rampant in Islamic Spain: Said al-Andalusi (d. 1070) taught a climatologically based inferiority of black Africans. Similarly, the scholar Ibn Khaldun (1332- 1406) leaves no doubt about the sub-humanity of blacks:

"*Therefore, as a rule, black peoples are submissive to slavery, for they have little that is human and have qualities quite similar to those of dumb animals, as we have noted*".

During the trans-Saharan slave trade, slaves from West Africa were transported across the Sahara desert to North Africa to be sold in Mediterranean and Middle eastern slave markets along with slaves from central Asia and Europe. The Indian Ocean or east African slave trade, was multi-directional. Africans were sent as slaves to the Arabian Peninsula, to Indian Ocean islands (including Madagascar), to the Indian subcontinent, and later to the Americas. These traders captured Bantu peoples (Zanj) from the interior in present-day Kenya, Mozambique and Tanzania and brought them to the coast.

A large number of Africans who were enslaved were not "exported", but were kept in domestic slavery. For example in the Senegambia region, between 1300 and 1900, close to one-third of the population was enslaved. In early Islamic states of the western Sahel, including Ghana, Mali, Segou, and Songhai, about a third of the population were enslaved.

As recently as the early 1960s, Saudi Arabia's slave population was estimated at 300,000. Along with Yemen, the Saudis abolished slavery in 1962. Historically, slaves in the Arab World came from many different regions, including Sub-Saharan Africa (mainly Zanj), the Caucasus (mainly Circassians), Central Asia (mainly Tartars), and Central and Eastern Europe (mainly Slavs).

The world owes the abolition of slavery to European culture, in particular the British were very active in this respect. After several centuries during which slavery was banned in some European countries while being permitted in overseas territories, a pukka effort to eradicate slavery around the world was finally made as from the early 19th century.

The Slave Trade Act was passed by the British Parliament on March 25, 1807, making the slave trade illegal throughout the British Empire, and with the Slavery Abolition Act in 1833 slavery was abolished in the British Empire.

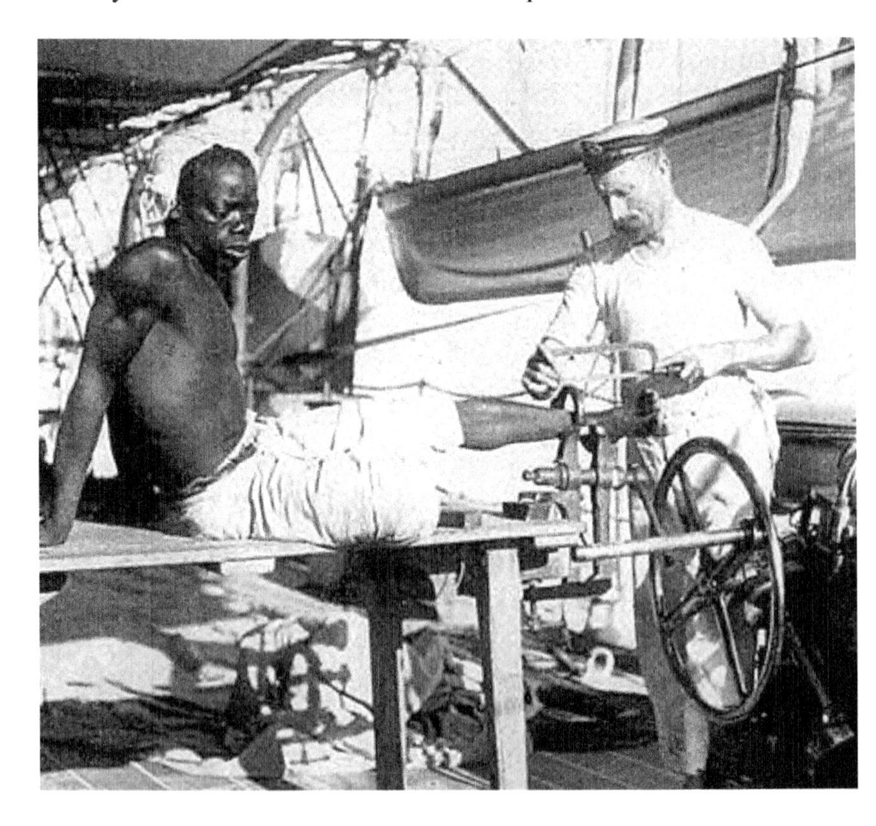

Freeing a slave rescued from Arab slave traders from his shackle on HMS Sphinx off the East Coast of Africa 1907

The Royal Navy and the Battle to End Slavery

After the 1807 act abolishing the slave trade was passed, these campaigners switched to encouraging other countries to follow suit, notably France and the British colonies. Between 1808 and 1860, the British West Africa Squadron alone seized approximately 1,600 slave ships and freed 150,000 Africans who were aboard. British captains caught transporting slaves were hanged. Around 90% of the effort to suppress the slave trade was borne by the British who used about 15% of their navy ships for this purpose; the cost roughly equalled the amount British slave traders had earned before from slavery. At its peak in the 1840s and 1850s, British operations off the West African coast involved up to 36 vessels and more than 4,000 men, costing an estimated half of all naval spending – amounting to between 1% and 2% of British government expenditure. The cost to the Royal Navy was heavy: one sailor died for every nine slaves freed – 17,000 men over the 52-year period – either in action or of disease.

The constant pressure of the British navy, however, was perceived by other countries as a breach of international law and national sovereignty. Indeed, the abolitionists pushed for direct imperial intervention. For decades, British warships provided humanitarian intervention, making Britain the world's policeman.

In 1841, a multilateral treaty was signed which put the slave trade on a par with piracy and provided for the surveillance of the world's oceans and the imposition of naval blockades - in the service of humanity. After that, up to 60 warships regularly patrolled African waters, mainly British, but also French and American.

Action was also taken against African leaders who refused to agree to British treaties to outlaw the trade, for example against "the usurping King of Lagos", deposed in 1851. Anti-slavery treaties were signed with over 50 African rulers.

In 1839, the world's oldest international human rights organization, Anti-Slavery International, was formed in Britain by Joseph Sturge, which campaigned to outlaw slavery in other countries. There were celebrations in 2007 to commemorate the 200th anniversary of the abolition of the slave trade in the United Kingdom through the work of the British Anti-Slavery Society.

In the 1860s, David Livingstone's reports of atrocities within the Arab slave trade in Africa stirred up the interest of the British public, reviving the flagging abolitionist movement. The Royal Navy throughout the 1870s attempted to suppress "this abominable Eastern trade", at Zanzibar in particular.

British sailors and slaves rescued by HMS Racoon from Arab slave traders in November 1868.

Kroo Sailors

The Kroomen came from the coast along today's south-east Liberia, where a small tribe shared the Kroo language and a clutch of small villages. Yet their identity as a nation or community was inextricably linked to the rise of European trading along the West African coast and, more importantly, the history of the British Preventative Squadron. The history of anti-slavery patrolling is at the essence of what made a Krooman a Krooman.

Kroo speakers were expert navigators and boatmen who piloted canoes made to ride over the coastline's high surf. When European vessels appeared in West African waters, the Kroo approached them to trade.

From the late 1700s, European and American ships started taking the Kroomen aboard to serve as pilots, interpreters or scouts. Eventually, the Kroomen became capable of running the ship themselves. 'Fifteen minutes after firing the bow gun the Kroo boys began to come off their canoes', wrote the English trader Alfred Smith. 'The crew of the good ship Angola were now replaced by Kroo boys, who handled everything like born sailors and replaced the whites, who were put to work on easier jobs like washing winches, splicing ropes.'

By the early 1830s, when the West African squadron came into its heyday, a fierce opposition to the slave trade had become part of Kroomen's identity, partly because of their high-status work for the Royal Navy's anti-slavery patrols and in part because they believed that Kroomen could not be slaves. 'White man no slave, Krooman no slave', went a saying of theirs.

Krooman in the Royal Navy

East Africa's slave hub – Zanzibar

The slave trade in East Africa really took off from the 17th century. More and more merchants from Arabia settled in Zanzibar. The island took on an even more important role in the international trade of goods due to the large trade at the Swahili coast and consequently also in the slave trade. This is how the largest slave market in East Africa was created.

Only estimates, some of which vary widely, exist as to how many Africans were sold from East to North Africa. This is also due to the fact that many of the slaves perished. Scientific research concludes that about three out of four slaves died before they reached the market where they were to be sold. The causes were hunger, illness or exhaustion after long journeys.

David Livingston, a Scottish missionary and explorer, estimated that 50,000 slaves were being sold annually in the markets of Zanzibar.

However, it was not until 1873 that Sultan Seyyid Barghash of Zanzibar, under pressure from Great Britain, signed a treaty that made the slave trade in his territories illegal. That decree was not enforced effectively either. It was not until 1909 that slavery was finally abolished in East Africa.

Chained slave women in Zanzibar

Zanzibar about 1890. The child is being held for sale as a slave. The child is chained to the heavy piece of lumber to restrict his or her movement, but movement is possible by carrying the heavy lumber. The pad on the head suggests the child is being trained to carry heavy items. The British Royal Navy by this time had substantially reduced the Indian Ocean slave trade, but because of the continuing demand for slaves in Arab markets was unable to completely end it.

Humanitarian colonialism - abolition in Africa

The struggle against slavery revealed deep rifts between cultures. The widest gaps were between countries of transatlantic Western culture and those that were heavily influenced by Islam. In the American ex-colonies, individual factions of the indigenous elites pushed for abolition - for example in Chile, Mexico or Argentina - acting within a state-institutional framework: if slavery was abolished, it remained so. It was different in the Islamic world, especially in its Arabised parts.

The major slave-importing areas besides Brazil and the Caribbean were the Maghreb, the Ottoman Empire – especially its Arab parts – and Persia. The British pressured the Turkish government for decades to stop the slave trade; the government left it at proclamations, which were hardly followed by action. The Arabian Peninsula was threatened with revolts because of the impending ban, so the Ottoman government exempted them from the ban in 1857. As it became increasingly clear that the Islamic countries would never abolish slavery outright on their own, the British had to cut off the supply. Their fleet now had to operate in the Indian Ocean in much the same way as it had for 60 years in the Atlantic. Only when they occupied Egypt in 1882 did they succeed in drying up the slave trade in the Middle East, except for the continuing flow across the Red Sea.

In Africa, abolition had to be imposed on the elites by force. Not only because the local elites profited from enslavement and the slave trade and slavery, but because the state structures were based on permanent enslavement; therefore the enslavement wars continued and covered larger areas in Central Africa. The British abolitionists had expected that "legitimate trade" – European imports of African agricultural products, especially oils – would bring the slave trade and slavery to an end. Instead, the slave plantations that produced these export goods expanded in West Africa. Now the abolitionists were pushing hard to stop the enslavement in the largest supply zone of the globe, if necessary by military means. It was high time. In the meantime, the enslavement wars had also spread to the Congo Basin and eastern Central Africa; on the one hand, because the Brazilian slave trade was supplied here, and on the other hand, because the Arab slave hunters reached the area of the Great Lakes up the Nile at the beginning of the 19th century and thus the hunting grounds of the Swahili Arab emirates on the East African coast. The intensification of the plantation economy around Malindi and Mombasa required a constant supply of slaves, especially the cultivation of cloves on the plantations of the islands of Pemba and Zanzibar, which the Arabs practised on a Caribbean scale and which required an oversized supply of slaves because of the high death rates – up to 30% per year. Warlords like

Tippoo Tip and Mirambo established themselves in these areas from Uganda to Lake Malawi, and went on to create slave-hunting emirates. The European colonial powers crushed these attempts.

More books by Arthur Lee Knight

Ronald Hallifax; or, He would be a Sailor, etc.

In the Web of Destiny;
or, the Strange Adventures of Lieut. Fairlie, R.N.

The Adventures of a Midshipmite

The Mids of the "Rattlesnake": or, Thrilling Adventures with Illanun Pirates, and Ned Burton's Adventures in the Fiji Islands

Dicky Beaumont: his Perils and Adventures

Basil Woollcombe, Midshipman.

The Rajah of Monkey Island

The Cruise of the "Cormorant" or Treasure-Seekers of the

Orient

The Brother Middies; and Slavers, Ahoy!

Adventures of a Gunroom Monkey

In Jungle and Kraal

Leaves from a Middy's Log

A Mid of the Naval Brigade

Under the White Ensign; or, for Queen and Empire

The Young Rajah

A Sea-King's Midshipman

Drifted to Sea

The Mad Interpreter

Aubrey Vernon. A midshipman's Adventures

Two midshipmen are on shore leave in Colombo in Ceylon. When they see a monkey in a shop they decide to buy it. Thus begins the proud service of a monkey on board the British corvette Bullfrog. With the help of the monkey – not to mention a dog and some other animals on board – the Royal Navy takes on pirates and perils galore.

The humorous and exciting adventures of a gunroom monkey and his friend the dog have been popular with several generations of readers since they were first published in 1894 and continue to enchant young and old to this day.

General Francois Fohne is plotting a revolution in Haiti. With the help of a voodoo priest, a fanatic called Napoleon and an old pirate treasure, he is hoping to take over power and make himself the new president. But the only Haitian warship has a British captain. A web of intrigue is spun and brutal fighting unleashed, pitting Napoleon against a fat Haitian officer and British midshipmen against voodoo magic and savage revolutionaries. Will the general prevail? How will the Royal Navy react when the revolutionaries seek to get the pirate treasure from Cayman Island, a British Territory?

Printed in Great Britain
by Amazon